SALTWATER SUMMER

RODERICK HAIG-BROWN

**HARBOUR
PUBLISHING**

Harbour Publishing Co. Ltd.
P.O. Box 219, Madeira Park, BC
Canada V0N 2H0
www.harbourpublishing.com

Cover photograph from iStockphoto
Cover design by Teresa Karbashewski
Text design by Mary White
Printed and bound in Canada

 Canada Council Conseil des Arts
for the Arts du Canada

 BRITISH COLUMBIA
ARTS COUNCIL
An agency of the Province of British Columbia

Harbour Publishing acknowledges financial support from the Government of Canada through the Canada Book Fund and the Canada Council for the Arts, and from the Province of British Columbia through the BC Arts Council and the Book Publishing Tax Credit.

Library and Archives Canada Cataloguing in Publication

Haig-Brown, Roderick L., 1908–1976
  Saltwater summer / Roderick L. Haig-Brown.
  ISBN 978-1-55017-609-4

      I. Title.
PS8515.A3S3 2013   jC813'.52   C2013-900207-3

1

Don Morgan climbed out of the small cockpit of his boat, the *Mallard*, and walked forward to the pilothouse. He stood on the deck, with his back to the doorway of the pilothouse, looking southward over the Gulf of Georgia, the wide reach of water that separates Vancouver Island from the mainland of British Columbia. It was a perfect June day, full of sun, with a westerly breeze just lively enough to break an occasional whitecap on the blue water. The *Mallard*'s heavy-duty engine beat smoothly at trolling speed in easy alternation of its two cylinders. Her trolling poles were spread and her lines were all working-four astern, two from the bow poles. Six months earlier this would have been the picture of everything Don wanted for himself. Now almost nothing about it was good.

Don kicked at the nearest hatch cover, then stepped up on to it and looked about him at the other boats of the salmon fleet. The fishing had been poor since the start of the season and they were widely scattered, searching everywhere for the feeding schools of blueback salmon. He saw Nels Larsen creeping close along the shore of Vancouver Island, poking the square-cut bow of his heavy boat into every tidal eddy. As always, a dozen or more boats were keeping close enough to Nels to see if he found fish. Tubby Miller's little *Sea-Witch* was to the east, close by Rock Island; Old Man Drew Mikelson was near him, and two or three other boats. One of them, Don saw, was Art Hedley's big *Blue Heron*. While Tubby's little boat pitched almost hurriedly in the chop of the light westerly, the *Blue Heron* rode like a great white swan with scarcely a dip of her long trolling poles and only the slightest lift of her high bow. That, Don told himself for the hundredth time, was a boat. She belonged on the west coast of Vancouver Island, out on the open Pacific with the deep-sea trollers, not here in the inside waters. And that was where Art would be taking her in a few days.

For the first time since the start of the season a couple of weeks earlier, Don felt that there was no real hope of finding fish. He wanted to talk to someone. Deliberately he pulled in his lines, automatically checking the hook on each small, bright spoon as he slipped it into the wooden tub of salt water on the stern of his boat. The thought that had been in the back of his mind through the last few days of slow fishing became for the first time a solid conviction: it was going to be a poor year for bluebacks. Ordinarily that would not have been enough to depress him. Now it was.

He went forward again from the cockpit, raised his trolling poles upright against the mast, then dived down into the pilothouse to speed up his engine. As the *Mallard* settled her stern and began to pick up speed, he felt for a moment the strong pride of owning her, of being free to fish out the summer with her anywhere along the length of the British Columbia coast, from the American boundary north to Prince Rupert and Alaska. The *Mallard* had been his for just over three months, since the triumphant end of his first trapping season in Starbuck Valley the previous winter. She was a man-size boat, thirty-two feet long, beamy enough, and as thoroughly seaworthy as any boat of her size. She had a good pilothouse with heavy plate glass windows, a two-cylinder heavy-duty marine engine that gave her about eight knots, two bunks forward surrounded by well-built lockers; and, for the type of boat she was, she had a reasonably comfortable living room. Any fisherman, let alone a boy not yet seventeen, might well have been proud to own her. But Don was remembering that she was no longer a free boat. Old Mr. Shenrock of Bluff Harbor had had a good solid claim in her for something over a month now, a claim that had to be paid off before the end of the trolling season in September.

Don knew he wanted to talk to someone and he knew there was no one he would rather talk to than Tubby Miller, his close friend through the years at Bluff Harbor School and his trapping partner during the previous winter. Tubby might not have the answers, but at least Tubby would listen and understand.

Don slowed the *Mallard*'s engine again and stepped out on deck as he came level with Tubby's little boat. Tubby was sprawled in the stern, his feet on the starboard gunwale, his broad face red in the sun.

"Catching anything?" Don asked him across the space between the boats. Tubby grinned, shook his head, and held out both hands, palms down. Don asked, "Think you're going to?"

Again Tubby shook his head. "No. They hit first off, but we can't find 'em again." "Take in your lines," Don said. "It's time for a mug-up." In a few minutes Tubby's lines were in and the *Sea-Witch* was tied alongside the *Mallard*. Old Man Mikelson took in his lines and came over to tie along the other side of the *Mallard*. He came aboard, shaking his head gloomily at Don and Tubby. "Never saw a season like it," he said. "No boats getting fish. She's a bad one."

"This evening, maybe?" Tubby asked.

"I don't think so," the old man said. "Not all this week. Next week, when the tides get bigger, maybe. Only maybe."

Don went down in the cabin to shake up the stove. The water was boiling and he made fresh coffee. He poured three cups and brought them up on deck with a frying pan full of ham slices and some bread. They settled themselves comfortably and began to eat.

The three boats were heading straight up the gulf, tied together so that the *Mallard*'s rudder controlled them. All three motors were running lazily, with little more than speed enough to hold them in place against tide and breeze, an unspoken admission by their owners that they were tied together for no more definite purpose than conference.

They ate in silence for a few minutes, then Don said, "Do you really think it's going to be an off year for bluebacks, Mr. Mikelson?"

The old man didn't hurry to answer. He looked about him at the other boats that were still fishing, his blue eyes distant and thoughtful, his lined face thin and sharp in the bright light. He looked far away to the mainland mountains and let his mind work back through the stored knowledge of forty seasons of hope and disappointment, success and failure, searching for some echo of circumstances and conditions that would let him speak positively. He found none, but he said at last: "It's a mighty hard thing to say for sure. Some years there's fish, but they come late, later than this. Some years there's fish like we got now, spread all over so nobody gets a good catch and high boat's a different man every day. Mostly that's a sign it's a poor season all through. But it ain't for certain. Nothing about fish is for certain."

Don wanted to pin him down tighter than that. "If you knew a man had to make her pay this season, would you say he'd better go some place else than the Gulf?"

The old man answered without hesitation. "Inside waters is no place for a young fellow with a good boat." He waved a hand vaguely over the *Mallard*. "Inside waters is for old men and farmers. If I was a young man again I wouldn't be here, no matter if the whole gulf was jumping with bluebacks clear from Cape Mudge to the mouth of the Fraser."

Don smiled. "Guess I'd stick around if she looked that good. But the way she is now I've got to get out of here and make a dollar someplace else. I haven't much more than made grub and gas the last couple of weeks."

"Me neither," Tubby said. "But I don't care too much. It'll pick up some as the season goes on. I thought that was the way you felt about it too, Don. You said so long as you could clear enough to rig the boat with steel lines and gurdey spools for next season you didn't mind sticking around inside. I might've known you'd get ambitious all of a sudden, though."

"It was different when I told you that," Don said. "Now, if I don't make her pay this season I won't have a boat to rig with gurdies and steel lines for next season."

Tubby sat up straight, his cheerful face suddenly worried. "How come? She's paid for, isn't she?"

Old Mikelson laughed. "Sure, she was paid for. But now she's got to be paid for over again. That's right, ain't it, Don? Never you mind though, you'll make it. You're not the kind that loses out."

Don looked at the old man in surprise. "How did you hear about it?" he asked. "I haven't told anyone yet."

"Things like that get out," Mikelson said. "Fishermen have long ears for what happens to boats." He turned and spoke directly to Tubby. "When Doc Hale told Lee Jetson last spring he was real sick and had to go to town for an operation and a whole lot of treatment, Lee said he didn't have the money. Said he guessed he'd just as soon die anyway. Doc told Don here and Don couldn't see it like that. So he went along and borrowed all the money old Shenrock'd lend him against the *Mallard*. Ain't that right, Don?" Don nodded and Mikelson went on. "And the paper says it's to be paid in full by September thirtieth next or Shenrock can take the boat and sell her to the highest bidder."

"That's right," Don said. "But I don't see how you know all about it."

"Seen all kinds of 'em. In the depression half the fishermen around here used to start out the season with a paper like that. I've done it myself. There ain't so many now, but I didn't figure old Shenrock'd change it none."

"Gee," Tubby said. "You sure are crazy, Don."

"Nothing so crazy about that," Mikelson said. "Helping out a partner when he's up against it. But Don'll have to get out and rustle if he wants his boat back. He won't make her inside, not this season."

Tubby said, "What are you going to do, Don?"

"Head north," Don told him. "Right away."

Old Mikelson looked hard at him, squinting his eyes almost closed in the sunlight. Inside him he seemed to be laughing at something. "North," he said gently. "But where to? A man needs to know where to, even if he don't git there in the end."

"What does that mean?" Don asked.

"It means, don't make a fish-boat bum out of yourself. Don't burn up gas and time running from one place to another looking for fish all season long like some of them do."

Tubby nodded. "That's right. That's what a lot of 'em do and it's easy enough to understand, at that."

"I'd go to the West Coast," Don said. "But I'd sooner wait till I've got the boat rigged right and know a bit more about it. The way it is, I figure now I'll head right up to Pendennis Island and work south from there."

"That's sound sense," the old man said. "You'd better take a partner. And stop in at the river before you start out. Joe and Maud Morgan'd be after my hide if they thought I'd talked you into this."

Don grinned. "Aunt Maud's not so tough as you guys like to think. But don't worry, I'll be stopping by there." He picked up the cups and the frying pan. "Cut loose, Tubby. I'm on my way right now."

"I'm coming in with you," Tubby said. "I haven't been home for a week." Old Mikelson loosed the stem line of his own boat. "So long, boys," he said. "I'll see you next fall."

2

Tubby Miller stood in the pilothouse of the *Mallard*, his hand on the wheel, his eyes staring thoughtfully out at the empty water ahead. He could hear Don below him, pumping water into the sink and clattering dishes as he washed them. Tubby had the *Mallard* on three-quarter throttle, where she cruised best. His own little *Sea-Witch* was securely tied alongside, her single cylinder doing its share of the work. Tubby was making up his mind; or rather, he had made up his mind and he was working out the details. They were complicated details and he had to work fast, sort them all out before Don finished the dishes and came up on deck. Tubby hoped he would take time to straighten up the cabin before he came.

Tubby had known old Mikelson all his life and he knew that everything the old man had said to Don had been seriously meant. More than that. Tubby knew he had left some things unsaid and that they were important things. For instance, that Shenrock, though fair enough in his way, was a dangerous man to deal with—he played for keeps and wasn't interested in the other guy's hard luck. Mikelson figured Don had to go outside to be sure of paying off the debt on the *Mallard*, but at the same time he realized that the *Mallard* wasn't any more than enough boat for outside and Don hadn't any experience to spare. That was why Mikelson had made that crack about taking a partner and it was where Tubby's decision came in. In all their affairs together Don had always been the leader, the one who had the ideas and got things done. But on the salt water, around boats and as a fisherman, Tubby knew that he had far more experience than Don.

His mind was made up to go north with Don. Though he had come to it quickly, this had not been an easy decision. Tubby liked his little boat and his own easygoing way of doing things. He liked the men he fished with in the inside waters and he liked being within reach of his home at Bluff Harbor.

When you go along with Don, Tubby told himself, you run into trouble and hard work, too much excitement usually and far too much discomfort. True, he always seemed to come out on top of things in the end and you were up there with him when he did. But that wasn't why Tubby was going north. It was because Don was Don, someone you liked even when you were mad at him, someone you had shared a lot of things with and had talked your most private thoughts to. It wasn't really a decision, it was just something natural. Decisions were things like what to do with the *Sea-Witch* and how to tell the old man, and Tubby thought he had those pretty well figured out.

Don came up into the pilothouse and stood beside him without speaking, but Tubby could sense that he was eager and excited. Tubby said, "How soon are you pulling out, Don?"

"Soon as I can make it. We can sell the fish we've got at the cannery, I'll take on gas and water there, then run up the river to see the folks. Ought to be able to pull out and catch the tide through the Narrows tomorrow morning." He stepped out on deck and stood looking back at the Gulf. "Kind of hate to leave it, at that. I'd got used to the idea of putting in the summer here. And I'm going to miss the old *Sea-Witch* tied alongside when it's time to head for home."

Tubby knew Don would never ask him to go along, if only because of the *Sea-Witch*. If a man owned a boat that could catch fish, even a little boat like the *Sea-Witch*, you didn't ask him to go off and leave her. That was the size of the thing he was going to offer and he knew he had to make it sound casual, a favor asked rather than a favor offered, or Don would turn him down. So he said, "How's chances to tag along?"

"I wish the heck you could. But I don't see how. You couldn't really take the *Sea-Witch* outside; it wouldn't pay because there'd be too many days you couldn't fish."

"I don't mean take her. I mean go with you as crew." Don turned sharply round and faced him. "You mean you'd do that? As partner, not crew." "As crew," Tubby said. "One-third share. That leaves one for you and one for the boat."

"Partners. Fifty-fifty or not at all."

Tubby shrugged his shoulders. "Okay. Partners it is."

Don held out his hand and they shook on it, solemnly and contentedly. "What'll you do with the *Sea-Witch*?" Don asked.

"Dave wants her. He hasn't got the dough, but he said he'd pay something down and thirty bucks a month to buy her on charter."

Don looked at the neat lines of the little boat, at the gleaming paint and tidy gear. "'Tain't right," he said awkwardly. "Dave's not the guy for a boat like that. He'll never pay for her, either." His voice changed suddenly. "Look, Tub, couldn't we run up there together, like this, and you fish her on good days and come out with me in the *Mallard* on bad days?"

"No. That way we'd gum up everything. Dave can have her. I'm due for a bigger boat next season anyway."

It was late afternoon when Don rounded the point on his way out of Bluff Harbor and swung north towards the mouth of Starbuck River. He had gas and grub and water aboard and had squared his account with the cannery with five dollars left over. Jim Avery had paid him off in the office and had said: "You're smart to take the *Mallard* north, Don. You'll find fish somewhere up there. It's going to be a bad year down here."

"Sure," Don had said. "But five bucks isn't much of a stake to start out with."

"You'll make out. Fishermen always do."

Don smiled as he felt the crumpled bill in his pocket. Uncle Joe and Aunt Maud wouldn't think much of a guy starting out with five bucks, but Jim was right. That was the way fishermen did, often as not, and they always seemed to make out some way. Don felt fine. He had not really wanted to fish another season in the inside waters and had decided to do so only because Joe Morgan, his uncle and guardian, had asked him to give it a fair trial first, and because he knew he could afford to have another season's experience behind him before trying the outside. The poor opening weeks of the blueback season, coming so soon after he had mortgaged his boat to Shenrock, had shown him the weight of the debt he had taken on as nothing else could have. But by fishing steadily through the bad weeks he had fulfilled his bargain with Joe Morgan and was free to try the outside. The thought was exciting in a way that he liked above all others. It meant unknown and untried difficulties in new waters among men he admired, and a test of his fitness to be among those men. That Tubby was coming along made the whole thing perfect. Between Don and Tubby there was a bond of shared experience far stronger than mere friendship and this, far more than the sea experience Tubby would bring to the venture, was what counted. On that evening it did not cross Don's mind that they might have as much difficulty in finding fish up north as they had in the Gulf. He had put troubles of that sort behind him as he took the cannery's five-dollar bill from Jim Avery.

There was plenty of tide when he came to the river and he ran the *Mallard* easily up the mile or so of smooth water to the pool by Joe Morgan's farm. They had heard the sound of his motor long before he got there and Joe Morgan was sliding the canoe into the water as Don killed his motor and dropped anchor. As the motor died, he could hear only the sound of the rapid at the head of the pool. The *Mallard* drifted gently backward in the current and came tight on her anchor chain. The ripples of her passage up the river caught up to her in smooth, glassy rolls that spread to the shore on either side. Don realized that he was glad to be away from salt water for a little while, glad to escape for at least one night from the narrow quarters of his boat.

Joe Morgan brought the canoe alongside and Don dropped smoothly down into it from the *Mallard's* gunwale. "How's everyone?" he asked.

"Fine," Joe said. "Ray and Ellen are here. Your aunt'll be glad to see you. How's the fishing?"

"Bad," Don told him. "We haven't even made grub out there for the last week."

"That's what I heard. I was hoping it might have picked up." And for the time being they left it at that, though Joe knew Don hadn't come back in the middle of the week simply because of a poor spell of fishing.

Aunt Maud met them at the back door. She was a big woman, seeming twice the size of her short, spare husband, direct in her speech, and very positive in all her movements. For years after he came to live in her house Don had been afraid of her direct ways and her outspokenness, but now he knew her well and trusted her as fully as he trusted Joe Morgan. "Well, Don," Maud said. "What brings you here in the middle of the week? Something serious or is it just you want a decent meal for a change?"

Don laughed. "I can eat anything you've got, Aunt Maud," he said. "But I guess there's trouble too, kind of."

"Going north, I suppose," she said. "Like all fishermen, never satisfied with where you are. Come on in and tell us about it. Supper's on the table."

Don's cousin, Ellen, was inside with Ray Baxter. They had been married for little more than a month and were on their way back to Ray's cabin on Starbuck Lake after a honeymoon in Vancouver. Don was fond of them both and glad of the chance to see them.

It was one of Aunt Maud's great suppers, a fine leg of lamb with green peas and new potatoes that she had forced ahead of their time in the special part of the garden that Joe Morgan was never allowed to touch. They talked the talk of a reunited family, the small things that would have been shared as they happened but for the separation.

Ray had seen Lee Jetson in town. "They've got him in bed still, but he's coming fine. Said to tell you and Tubby he'd write soon and that he'd be back working on the claims long before snow flies."

Don asked, "Will he really get better? No kidding?"

"The doctors say they've fixed him up," Ray said. "And he'll be good as he ever was as soon as he's up and about again."

"That's a big thing," Joe Morgan said. "I couldn't stand to see that man hit any more tough luck than he's had."

"I've never seen him look so happy," Ellen said. "He told Ray a man doesn't know what friends are until he's in real trouble. He meant it about you, Don."

Don said nothing and in a little while they began to talk of the fishing and his decision to go north. Ray Baxter and Joe Morgan supported it; Aunt Maud said again that it was nothing more than a fisherman's restlessness, but she seemed to accept it, as she had been accepting all her life what she felt was the shiftlessness of the whole male sex, with a despairing tolerance. It was only later in the evening that Don fancied she was watching him closely, following every word he said in a way that she never had before. Their eyes met and there was something in his aunt's look that made Don cross the room to her. He stood awkwardly beside her for a moment, then he said: "I guess I'd better hit the hay. Tubby'll be along first thing tomorrow."

After he had gone upstairs Maud Morgan said: "That boy is carrying too much load for a youngster. 'Tain't right."

"He'll make out," Joe Morgan said. "With Tubby along they'll handle anything that comes up, just the way they did up the valley last winter."

"Don's worried," Ellen said. "He's not like himself. He's glad he's going, but he's scared of something, too."

"Sure he is," Maud said. "Didn't you know he had tied that boat of his up to Mr. Shenrock for Lee Jetson's operation? He hasn't told us, but we know that's what he's done."

"That's right," Ray said. "Lee told me." "Lee shouldn't have taken it," Maud said. "And you should take the load off'n him now, Joe."

Joe Morgan reached in his pocket for his pipe. "Lee didn't have any choice," he said. "And Don wants to carry his own load. If he didn't he'd say so. He's more man right now than most men ever get to be, and he didn't get that way without carrying his own loads."

"Children," Maud said disgustedly. "They're both kids. Going up there into all that bad water and not a soul to look out for them." But she left it at that, and it was not her way to leave things if she thought she could do anything about them.

3

Don went out to help his uncle milk before breakfast the next morning. Coming back from the barn Joe Morgan said, "If things get tough while you're up there, don't ever forget you've got lots of friends."

"I know that, Uncle Joe," Don said simply. "But I don't reckon a man should call on his friends without he has to."

"That's up to you, but don't ever forget we're here. Mind if I say something, Don? Kind of advice, the way I used to talk when you were younger?"

Don stopped in the pathway, holding the two full pails. "Heck, no, Uncle Joe. Why should I?"

"Well, it's this. Last winter, when you and Tubby went trapping together, you had a whole lot to look out for. But they was all nature things, rivers and weather and the woods and animals.

Those things can do you dirt if you don't handle yourself right, but they're still pretty simple alongside men. This fishing'll bring you up against men, as well as all the rest. Most of 'em will be for you, a few will likely be against you. It's the ones that are for you that can do you the worst harm, if you ain't watching." Joe paused and set down the pails he was carrying. He was thinking hard, searching for words to say what he wanted in a way that Don would accept, and that was unusual for Joe Morgan, because he could nearly always say what he had to say easily and well. "Fishermen are the same as other men mostly," he went on at last. "There's good and bad in them. Most of them are steady and hard workers. But there's a lot of them are kind of heedless, too easygoing and good-natured for their own good. That's where a young fellow has to watch himself. Easygoing habits are easy to get into and there doesn't seem much harm in them. There isn't, so far as that goes, except for a man's own self."

He paused again and Don said, "I think I know what you mean all right, Uncle Joe, and I'll watch it."

"There's something else," Joe said. "Liquor. There's no harm in that either, if it's used right. But don't be in any hurry to start using it. The law says under twenty-one is too young for a man to start drinking and the law's dead right for once. There's never any reason for a young fellow to start drinking then, except he thinks it's a smart thing to do."

Don asked quietly, "When did you have your first drink, Uncle Joe?"

Joe's face relaxed and he laughed aloud. "Before I was twenty-one, I guess," he admitted. Then he was serious again. "But it wasn't more'n a glass of beer, at that. I was twenty-five and over before I tasted hard liquor and I reckon I still haven't drunk up as much money as many a man does in one year. I ain't worrying none about you," he added. "It's just I figure I ought to say what your dad would be saying to you if he was still alive."

Joe Morgan picked up his milk pails and they walked together back to the house.

Tubby arrived on time and they got a start from the river a good hour before high water slack. "Should make the Narrows fine," Tubby said.

Don did not answer. He was feeling the wrench of leaving Starbuck River, the Morgan farm, and the woods and logging works of the valley. It was a feeling that would be gone as soon as they were well on their way, he knew, but it was strong in him for the moment, not less strong because of the ten-dollar bill that Aunt Maud had slipped almost furtively into his hand as she said good-by. "It won't be much help," she had said. "But it'll buy something good to eat on the way."

They passed the bend by the big spruce tree and came in sight of salt water. A trolling boat was anchored just inside the mouth of the river. "Who's that?" Don asked.

"Don't know," Tubby said. "Never saw her before."

They studied the boat with fishermen's eagerness as they came closer to her. She was big, maybe thirty-eight feet, Tubby judged, with forty-foot poles and power gurdies to handle three lines on each side. A man came out on deck, dumped something overboard, and stood watching the *Mallard* as she came closer. He was a tall man, rangily built, yet heavy above the waistline, with dull red hair and a big handsome face. Probably about thirty years old, Tubby thought, and he weighs two hundred and ten or better. He read the name on the bow of the boat—*Falaise*.

The man waved as they came close and Don slowed his engine right down and kicked the clutch out. The man asked, "How's fishing, chums?"

"Not so hot," Tubby told him.

"What's your hurry then? Better tie up and have a cup of coffee."

Tubby started to say something about catching the tide in the Narrows, but Don kicked in the clutch and speeded up to circle and come back against the current. Tubby went up to the bow and picked up the line. "Your anchor hold us both in the current?" he asked.

"Sure thing. When Red Holiday puts an anchor out, it'll hold the *Queen Mary* in a gale."

They spoke their names and shook hands. "Partner's still asleep down below," Red told them. "Name of Moore, Tom Moore. They don't come any better. Where you fellows heading?"

"North," Don said. "Pendennis Island, I guess." He was admiring the bright steel lines on the gurdey reels and the whole workmanlike rigging of the boat. "Where're you heading?"

"I was figuring on the West Coast. But come to think of it, Tom and I are about due for a change. Why don't we go up to the Island, too? Haven't been up there since before the war. A guy can get into a rut if he goes to the same place all the time."

Tom Moore came up from below, a slender, dark man with black eyes and nervous hands. "Meet Don and Tubby, Tom," Holiday said. "We're all going north together."

"We better get going pretty soon," Tubby said. "Or we'll miss the slack water in the Narrows."

"Couldn't matter less," Red told him. "If we stop for a mug-up now, we'll get us a good boost through on the start of the ebb."

"And be bucking the flood by midafternoon," Don said.

"What's your rush?" Red asked. "We'll tie up as soon as she starts to get tough and run on the ebb again after dark."

They did it Red's way and came in sight of the Narrows a full hour after slack water. Don watched the swells and folds of current on the oily smooth water and felt the thrill he always felt in passing that place, where the powerful tides of the east coast of Vancouver Island crowd into a bare half mile of channel. He was standing with Red in the roomy pilothouse of the *Falaise*. The *Mallard* was tied alongside and Tubby and Tom Moore were both in their bunks. Don watched the steep shore line slip by faster and faster as the tide caught them. From time to time he glanced back at Red's intent face.

"Won't be very strong today," Red said without taking his eyes off the water. "We're still early for the best of it. Nothing much this side of Ripple Rock on the ebb anyway. We'll stay tied together." He spun the wheel to meet a sudden throw of unseen current and glanced quickly toward the high point south of Menzies Bay on the Vancouver Island shore. "You can run in fairly close to Race Point on the ebb. Keep right away from the darn place on the flood, though. I've seen boils of water there'd make you think the whole ocean's coming up at you from the bottom. Bad whirls, too. I'll take you up the steamer course this trip." Don watched Race Point slide by and saw Red ease the *Falaise*'s bow over toward Maud Island Light on the other shore. He felt the same elation he felt in running his canoe through a stretch of fast water in the Starbuck—a sense of power and control, yet an intense awareness of greater power, beyond control, all about him.

Red glanced toward him and grinned. "Makes a guy think, don't it? Makes you feel kind of small, but kind of good, too. There's lots worse places for a small boat than the old Seymours, but a guy gets a different feeling out of them."

It was a sparkling day, without a breath of wind, and no other boats were passing the Narrows at that time. Don watched the broken water beyond Ripple Rock. "The old Rock really kicks it up," he said. "But I should think a small boat'd handle it if a man didn't do anything crazy."

"He'd have to be crazy to go in there," Red said. "But you're probably right, at that. If a boat's a good model and you give her a fair chance, she'll handle almost anything in the way of rough water." They were passing Maud Island within two or three hundred feet, passing the shore at twice the *Falaise*'s top speed. The current swirled and pulled at them and Red moved the wheel constantly to meet the jolting shocks and twists. Suddenly the overfall of meeting currents was breaking white all about them in short, sharp little waves. The bow of the *Falaise* dipped, wrenched sharply over and Red pulled her back. Something slid across the floor of the cabin below them. "Better stand to your own boat till we see how it is," Red told Don. "I wouldn't want one of those lines to break. Leave the wheel alone though."

Don went out of the pilothouse and dropped down to the deck of the *Mallard*. Tubby came up from below. "Gee," he said. "We're taking an awful pitching around." Then he looked out at the broken water. "H'm," he added. "Not really bad, considering."

"No," said Don. "That guy's good. And he likes it." The edge of a whirl caught them and both boats heeled far over, righted, hit another whirl and heeled again. "Couple more like that," Tubby said judicially, "and something's liable to break loose. I better look" He went below again.

Don leaned against his pilothouse, watching the break over Ripple Rock behind them. The water was still rough, but they were through and away for the north. It would be three months or more before he saw the Narrows again and came back to his own part of the coast.

4

Through the afternoon they rode the ebb tide up the long reach of Discovery Passage. When the flood began to make against them they turned into a little bay, dropped anchor, and cooked supper. Red asked: "What do you guys figure on doing? Run straight through to Pendennis Island?"

"No," Don said. "We've got to stop on the way to fish for gas money. We thought we'd try Viscount Channel. Tubby fished there once before."

"You don't need to do that. The company'll give you credit for gas and grub when you get there."

"I know, but I'd as soon not start out in the hole. What do you say, Tubby?"

"That's right," Tubby said. "Credit's okay if you have to have it, but a guy might as well stay independent as long as he can."

Red laughed. "You're right," he said. "I've been in the hole too often not to know."

"You going to hit right through?" Don asked him.

Red looked at his partner. "May as well. What say, Tom?"

Tom Moore looked up from his food. "You call the shots, Red, and I'll be right with you. Never lost out that way yet."

Don realized that this was the first time they had heard the dark man speak more than a word or two since they had met him that morning. He noticed again the tremor that was always in Tom's long hands and fingers, whether they were moving or resting. Red had stopped eating to watch his partner with a smile that was faintly amused, strongly affectionate, yet had in it something of the protective, reassuring pride that a teacher shows in the performance of a good pupil.

"We always make it, Tom, don't we? And we always will."

Tom glanced up at him quickly, smiled, and turned back to his food again. They talked about other things. Red kidded Tubby gently about his love of boats and salt water and kidded them both for being inside fishermen, promising them a great future now that they had seen the light. Don listened and said his say, but he found himself watching Tom and wondering about the close friendship between him and Red. It seemed to Don that he had never seen men more different. Red was strong, quick, confident, full of life and laughter and easy talk; everything he did and the whole way he looked and moved and held himself seemed easy, powerful, and sure. Tom was short, withdrawn, frail, and shy. At first you scarcely noticed him, then you noticed him in spite of his quietness because he seemed so different and out of place. Don didn't know whether he liked him or not, but he felt inclined to like him because Red so clearly did. In the same way and for the same reason he withheld any final judgment on Tom's usefulness in the partnership between the two men.

After supper Don said, "When'll we pull out again, Red?"

"Around turn of tide. That way it'll be good daylight when we come opposite Viscount Channel and we can go into Sullivan's camp for fuel."

"Then somebody'd better get some sleep," Tubby said. Don laughed. "That's what you've been doing a good part of the day."

"No kidding," Red said. "Tubby's got something there. A fisherman should sleep whenever he gets the chance." He reached into a locker behind him and brought out a deck of cards. "Cut 'em. Low man takes the first two hours and we'll change every two hours after that." Tubby cut the low card, Don was next, Tom Moore was high. Red put a hand on his shoulder. "You can sleep easy, Tom. We should be in before your number comes up. Kind of tough on the crew of the *Mallard*, though."

"Wake me anyway," Tom said. "I like coming into a new place around daylight."

Don woke when Tubby's alarm went off. "I'll come and help you get the hook up," he said. "It's okay," Tubby told him. "Red said he'd come up and start his own engine."

Don pulled on a pair of pants anyway and went up with him. It was a clear night, with daylight still in the west and only the stronger stars showing. On the high slack water everything seemed very still and quiet. Don went up to the bow with Red when the motors were running and noticed that the anchor chain was pulling almost straight down. "Didn't leave a heck of a lot to spare, did we?" he asked.

"Sure didn't," Red agreed. "A fellow gets used to those little ten or twelve foot tides on the Gulf and forgets it can go up to twenty-four feet once he's north of the Narrows. Sort of thing it don't pay to forget too often."

They took up the anchor, Tubby kicked in the clutch, and the boats began to swing out toward the channel again. Don checked his own engine, then pulled off his pants and rolled back into his bunk.

He woke to feel Tubby's hand on his shoulder. "Okay," he said sleepily. "Be right up." "There's coffee on the stove," Tubby said and went back to the *Falaise*'s wheelhouse.

Don poured himself a cup of coffee and drank it as he dressed, listening to the sound of his engine. It was smooth and good, but then he had known that it would be because Tubby's concern for everything about the *Mallard* was at least as great as his own.

He found Tubby in the wheelhouse of the *Falaise*. "It's half an hour past the time," Tubby said. "Everything was going so good I hated to go down and disturb you. Better wake Red on time, though. He'll want to check his engine. We're coming up on Bear Point now. You can pick up Cracroft Light ahead if you watch for it."

"Okay," Don said. "I've got it." And Tubby left him and went below.

The moon had come up while Don was sleeping and its light was pale and cold on the smooth water. The tide was still running strongly with them. Don eased the wheel over gently until the boats began to turn to starboard, then touched them back on their course again. It felt good to be there alone in the wheelhouse, with the throaty sound of the *Falaise*'s diesel above him and the rustle of water past the hull when he stuck his head out of the pilothouse door. He saw the port light of a tug passing to the west of him, three white masthead lights above it showing that she was towing a boom of logs against the tide. Vaguely he wondered if her skipper could be hoping to catch the last of the flood through the Narrows. If so, she'd be passing the mouth of the Starbuck in the next morning's daylight, within a mile or two of Joe Morgan's farm.

The first hour had passed quickly. Don decided it was time to go down and check the *Mallard*'s engine again. The channel was clear, he knew, and the boats had shown little or no sign of wandering even when he left his hands off the *Falaise*'s wheel for several minutes at a stretch. But he hurried over his job and went back on deck as quickly as possible, because being down below when the boats were running gave him a blind feeling that he did not like.

He was still on the deck of the *Mallard* when he heard the sound. It was a human sound, he knew, but it caught at his throat and tensed his muscles like the first lone howl of a wolf pack. It came again, and there was pain in it and fear and Don knew it came from the *Falaise*. He started to move toward it, then stopped because it suddenly had become a voice speaking, a straining voice, urgent yet clear.

"I'm going, I tell you. Somebody's got to and I'm going."

The last words were shouted and close. Don leapt for the deck of the *Falaise*, saw a figure, black in the moonlight, burst from the wheelhouse. He grabbed, caught a blow in the face that shocked through his whole body, and found himself wrestling with a man. The man spoke as he fought with him and Don knew it was Tom Moore. "Let me go. I'm not crazy. There's nothing else to do."

Then Red's voice. "Hang on to him. For Pete's sake, hang on to him." Red was there, his great arms round Tom's chest, holding him tight. He was speaking gently. "Easy, Tom, old-timer. Easy, old kid. You've fixed 'em. You're okay We're all with you."

Don felt a shiver run through Tom Moore's body and Red's voice went on, tender and soft almost as a woman's. "Everything's jake now, Tom. The whole of B Company's here, and there was tanks with them. Come and get some sleep. There isn't a thing to worry about any more."

Don was standing up. He looked ahead and saw that the boats were still on course; he looked back again to Red and Tom. Tom was sobbing, great heaving sobs like a child in misery. "Gee, I'm sorry, Red. I've done it again. I thought I was over that stuff."

"It's nothing to worry about, old-timer. Come on down and get some sleep." As they passed Don, Red whispered to him: "Thanks, chum. I'll be up again in a few minutes."

They went below and Don went into the pilothouse and took the wheel again. His hands were shaking and he felt weak and sick. There had been terror in Tom's voice that had reached deep down into him and would not be shaken off. And there had been something beyond terror, something that made Don feel alone and shut out, yet ashamed of his nearness in that helpless sobbing that followed the struggle. He was glad when Red came back to the pilothouse.

"That was my fault," Red said. "I should have been watching out for it. How did he get past you?"

"I was down on the *Mallard*," Don told him. "What was he going to do?"

"He'd have gone overboard if you hadn't stopped him." Red was rolling a cigarette and Don could tell from his voice that the thing had shaken him. "That's the first time it's happened in over a year. I thought he was over it."

"What is it?" Don asked. "What happened?"

"I guess you'd call it a bad dream. You see, Tom's not like you and me—he's an educated guy. And he's kind of high-strung, always has been, and thoughtful. It wasn't enough so you'd notice it when I first knew him overseas. He just seemed quieter and wiser than the rest of us; he was, too, and every man in the platoon used to go to him with trouble of any kind."

"You mean you were in the same outfit with him? Infantry?"

"That's right. We both went on our feet and packed rifles. But Tom was what they used to call 'officer material.' He should have been an officer. Only trouble was he wouldn't take training seriously after the first. We all got sick of doing the same old thing over and over, always waiting and never going any place, but most of us called it a day's work for a day's pay. Tom couldn't take it like that and he let them see he couldn't. So on D-Day he was still only a buck private."

Red flipped his cigarette overboard and began to roll another. "When it came to fighting," he went on, "Tom was a different guy altogether. He was a soldier twenty-four hours a day and seven days a week. He worked at it like six men. He knew his stuff better than any of us and he never let up. He was wounded twice, not much but more than enough for most men to quit and go back; and he stayed up with us." Red paused again and Don said nothing because he wanted him to go on. "It isn't easy to understand if you weren't there. I'm pretty tough and things don't bother me the way they do

Tom. Guys like you and me aren't thinking heavy all the time like he was. But I'd pretty near had it before I got wounded, late on in August. Tom was still going then and going good. He was platoon sergeant and the last of the originals left. When I saw him again it was after VE-Day and we were both on leave from hospital. Tom was like he is now, kind of lost and weak and worn-out, thinking things down deep inside him that he never lets out."

"What happened to him?" Don asked.

Red shrugged his shoulders. "Just wore out, I guess. He was wounded bad in December '44 and he never came out of it right. He's healthy enough, I guess, but his head isn't right. That's why he has those dreams. There's something bad inside him he can't shake loose."

Don thought of the way he and Tubby had talked of the war, wanting to be over there in the fighting. This made it seem different and made him feel very young. "Will he get better, do you think?"

"He's better'n he was, right now. But he don't seem to come alive. Tom always was a deep-thinking man and a quiet man. But he liked good times and there was lots of things he believed in that he'd come right out and talk for. I've heard him talk like a preacher or a politician, only better, and everybody'd listen to him. He don't do that any more. Seems like he's empty. The doc down at Shaughnessy says he's best out fishing like this and I know he's easier with me around. But it don't seem right, not for a man like Tom was." He slid open one of the pilothouse windows and let in a flow of cool night air. "That dream of his. It's about Falaise, where we got into a tough spot and he got us out of it by running right at the Heinies firing a Bren gun. Something about that is what he can't cut loose from. He'll find it some day, and when he does he'll be okay again."

5

About an hour after sunrise Red went down to wake Tom. "He's slept long enough to get over it," he told Don. "And he likes early morning. Don't say anything about last night. He won't remember, anyway."

In a little while they came up together. Tom stood quietly in the pilothouse, looking out at the bright water of the channel and the rocky shore line on either side. Don watched his face and saw the strained lines relax in it. The boats ploughed toward a little tide rip, disturbing some scoter ducks which splashed and flew heavily away. Tom watched them almost eagerly and his tired eyes seemed alive for a moment. He turned to Red. "We're in good country again," he said. "We shouldn't ever go south in the fall."

"It's fine to say that now," Red told him. "But you'll be ready to hit town same as the rest of us when fall comes." He put a hand on the wheel. "Don, you better go wake Tubby. We put fresh coffee and the frying pan on the stove before we came up."

They came in to Sullivan's Camp before the breakfast dishes were out of the way. It was an untidy collection of buildings on log floats, tied in a sheltered bay near the entrance to Viscount Channel. Two or three trolling boats were tied to the floats and there was smoke coming from the stovepipe on the little floating store. They tied up within reach of the fuel lines and killed the engines. Timothy Sullivan came out of his store and stood looking the boats over. He was something over fifty years old, a hugely built man with a great paunch pushing out ahead of him, and he didn't take any unnecessary steps. Red called to him: "How's tricks, Tim? Any fish around?"

Mr. Sullivan lumbered a little way toward them and Don felt that he was a privileged spectator at a major undertaking. "'Bout same as usual, Red. How's it with you?"

"We wintered fair enough," Red told him. "On our way north this season for a change. They catching fish there?"

"Run of big bluebacks come in two-three days ago. Some boats been doing pretty fair."

Red turned to Don and Tubby. "Right up your alley. Tom and I aren't rigged right for bluebacks though, so I guess we'll keep right on agoin'."

Red fueled his boat and he and Tom pulled out on the tide. "Don't hang around here too long," he told Don as they left. 'We'll look for you up there inside a week or so. Make a killing while you're here."

Don and Tubby rigged the small blueback spoons on the *Mallard*'s lines while Mr. Sullivan sat in the sun and watched them. "Don't figure to fish 'em too deep, boys," he told them. "They ain't feedin' deep. And don't worry about keeping tight in with the big bunch of the boats. There's fish all through the channel and you're as liable to find 'em away from the bunch as any place."

Don twisted a short length of wire to a bright metal spoon about three inches long, checked the hook, and dropped the spoon into the wooden tub of salt water on the *Mallard*'s stern. "How many spoons are they fishing, Mr. Sullivan?"

"Anywheres up to seven on a line. Mostly four and five." Tim Sullivan took his pipe out of his mouth and spat into the water. "Don't know as I hold with this blueback fishing anyways. They's nothing but young cohoes and by August they'll weigh more'n twice what they do now. Seems a terrible waste to catch little fish three or four pounds when they could as easy be eight or ten pounds."

"Waiting till August'd make a short season," Tubby said. "They're mostly up the rivers by October. And they don't can so good then. A blueback is as red as a sockeye."

Sullivan spat again. "What's red?" he asked. "Nothing but selling talk. Don't taste no better. Only looks good to them as doesn't know better."

By midafternoon they were fishing. Tubby had had a hunch, based on an experience of the previous season, and they had run four or five miles up the channel from Sullivan's, resolutely passing boats of all kinds and sizes and shapes, though they saw that many were catching fish. At last Tubby said, "This is it," and Don slowed the engine to trolling speed. They let the poles down from the mast and put out the lines. The bell on the tip of the starboard pole jingled at once. Tubby shook his head. "Don't pull," he said. "See what gives first. He'll draw others, anyway."

The main part of the channel ran roughly east and west and it was no more than two or three hundred yards wide where they were fishing. Just ahead of them a large bay widened the channel southward. Across the mouth of the bay was an island and Tubby held the *Mallard* along the edge of the eddy that formed behind it.

"We made some good catches here on this kind of tide last year," he told Don. "There's never much inside the bay, but it's good outside the island sometimes."

They were both in the little cockpit at the stern of the boat. Tubby had a foot on the tiller and was watching the line of the rip ahead. Don saw the break of feeding fish outside them and the splatter of tiny needlefish jumping out ahead of the salmon. "They're here," he said. A bell jingled on the outside pole; then another, and something hit the inside line to starboard. They began to pull fish.

The bluebacks were big, as Tim Sullivan had said. Don judged that most of them weighed four or five pounds, and they were striking freely. "Let the outside lines fill up," Tubby said. "We'll just pull the others while it lasts." Don brought in the heavy cotton line fast, hand over hand. There was a fish on the first spoon. Don swung him in board, freed the hook, and felt another strike on the line as he did so. The third fish tore away from the hook at the surface, but the fourth spoon of the line hooked a fish as Don was hauling it up to check it.

Don paid out the complicated line again—the deepest spoon, its short wire leader, two fathoms of cuttyhunk, the rubber link, two pounds of lead. Then two fathoms of main line, a three-pound lead, and the next spoon on its own bobber of wire and cuttyhunk and rubber. Two fathoms more of main line, another lead, another spoon and bobber. Two more fathoms and the shallow spoon, its bobber set just above eight pounds of lead. Before he had time to let the last spoon down to its fishing depth he knew the line was filled up and he began to haul in again.

Then the flurry of taking was suddenly over. They were opposite the island now, away from its shelter. "They're all in the eddy," Don said. "We better get back there."

Tubby was already swinging the boat, slowly, to keep the lines from crossing and tangling in the current. Don reached over and pulled one of the outside lines. There was a fish on the first spoon, but the other three were empty. "That's what I thought," he said. "They're all taking right on top."

Tubby nodded. "I know. May as well shorten right up this time and see if we do any better."

They came back through the eddy, and again feeding fish broke near them and again for a brief spell they pulled fish as fast as they could handle the lines. Don raised a hatch cover and pitched the cockpit clear of the steel-blue and silver bodies, then sluiced it down with a bucket of water. "Not bad," he said. "Must be nearly two hundred pounds in there."

When they came through the eddy the third time the lines did not fill so fast and they noticed its shape was changing. The fourth time through they caught only two fish and the rip line at the edge of the eddy was no longer visible. "That's the works," Don said. "We've got to find them somewhere else now."

Tubby nodded. "It never does last long. Sometimes the other side of the channel is good towards slack water. We might try it."

Don began cleaning fish as Tubby angled the boat across the channel, still at trolling speed. They could see into the bay now and Don noticed a log boom and a shack on a float near the steep shore.

"Whose place is that?" he asked Tubby.

Tubby glanced into the bay. "Gee, that's Mike and Walter. Dad said he heard they'd moved. You remember, those handloggers I used to go and see last year, old friends of Dad's."

A bell jingled on a bow pole and Tubby began to pull in line. "Something heavy," he said. "Spring salmon, I guess."

The fish had taken the deepest spoon on the line. He surfaced thirty feet behind the boat and splashed violently. "Hope the hook holds," Tubby said and let him have a little line. Don picked up the gaff.

"May as well use this and make sure of him."

"Okay," Tubby said and brought the fish up to the surface within reach. Don sank the gaff and lifted.

Tubby clubbed the fish. "Twenty-five pounds or better," he said. "That's a break."

They were across the channel now and another boat was fishing close alongside them. Tubby said, "We've got to get these fish back to Sullivan's or we could go in and see Mike and Walter tonight."

"Guess that's right," Don said. "It wouldn't pay to keep them over." "Not without ice. Sullivan wouldn't take them if we did."

Don held up the spring salmon and shouted across to the fisherman in the other troller, "Any more around?"

The man shook his head. "I got one all day. Deep, on the bowline. Bluebacks was good on the afternoon tide, though."

"Will they take again tonight?"

The man shook his head again and reached for an outside line that had hooked a fish. "Not likely. Packer should be along, anyway."

"Packer?" Tubby asked him. "Out here?" "Should be," the man said. "He's generally around. Independent buyer."

The boats were drawing apart and Tubby let the gap widen. "Sounds okay," he said. "We can sell our fish and tie up in the bay tonight. How much do you figure we've got there?"

"Around fifty bucks," Don said. "And we'll get two good tides tomorrow. Should be able to go on our way the day after."

"Why hurry if the fishing stays good?"

Don thought for a moment. He knew he wanted to go, but he didn't know exactly why. To see new country, for one thing. Because the north seemed to promise big things. And, he suddenly realized, because he wanted to see more of Red Holiday. But he knew Tubby was right. If the fishing was good they ought to stay with it. "Maybe it won't," he said. "Blueback runs are always patchy."

6

The packer came up to them a little before sunset and Don and Tubby sold their fish. "Call it a day?" Don asked as the packer pulled away from them.

"You bet," Tubby said. "We'll run right in to Mike and Walter's. Grab the wheel and I'll clean up the boat a bit."

As they came into the bay Don could see that a man was sitting out on the float in front of the shack, though a light already showed in the window behind him. As they came closer he saw the man stand up, stretch himself, and shade his eyes to peer toward the *Mallard*. He was a big man with gray hair and a reddish face. He was wearing a heavy wool undershirt, stained rain-test pants, wool socks, and a pair of slippers. Rubbing against his legs was a huge blue-gray tomcat. Don slowed the engine for his landing and Tubby came past the pilothouse. "That's Mike," he said. 'Walter's a little guy."

Tubby called something to Mike as the *Mallard* came in, but Mike seemed not to recognize him. He looked down and spoke slowly to the gray cat. "Well, Babe, looks like we got company."

Don shut off the engine and stepped out on the float with the stern line. Mike had the bowline and Tubby was speaking again, his hand held out to Mike. "Okay to tie up with you folks for the night?" he asked.

Mike seemed to see him for the first time. "Why, it's Tubby Miller. Sure, Tubby, sure. You bet you can tie up, and welcome. Who's your friend and where'd you get the new boat?"

Tubby introduced Don, and Walter came out of the shack. He was half the size of Mike, probably about the same age, with the same lined and reddened face and neck, and the same kind of undershirt and stained pants. He held a tattered magazine in one hand and was peering over a pair of spectacles that seemed quite out of place on his sunburned nose.

Mike didn't look round at him, but spoke again to the gray cat, quite loudly.

"Seems like young Tubby Miller's come back to see us, Babe. Ain't been around in nearly a year. Brought a friend with him. New boat."

Walter's puzzled little face lightened and he came forward quickly. "Sure is good to see you, boy." He stopped and made a courtly little bow to Don. "And glad to welcome you to Killarney Bay." Don heard Mike snort, but Walter turned to Tubby again. "When did you last eat?" he asked. "Could ye do with a bite of supper now? How's your dad?"

Mike spoke again to the cat. "Seems like some folks never stop their tongues, don't it, Babe?"

Walter looked down at the cat, too, and it paced grandly toward him along the float log. "Seems like some folks don't know how to greet company, don't it, Babe?"

Don looked at Tubby and saw that he was smiling. "Come on inside," Mike said heartily. "There's coffee on the stove and we can have ham and eggs fried up in no time."

Don said awkwardly: "We ate while we were fishing. We don't need more'n a mug-up down on the boat before we turn in."

"Nonsense, nonsense!" Mike's big voice boomed ahead of them as he led the way into the shack. "Come on inside and make yourselves to home."

So they went in and Mike cooked up a great mess of ham and eggs and coffee and they swallowed it down gratefully. The inside of the shack was as neat and tidy as a hospital, everything about it clean and swept and painted and polished. Carefully fitted cupboards lined all the walls, the stove was gleaming black, a Coleman gas lamp burned brightly on the spotless white oilcloth that covered the table. Walter moved about the room, bringing plates and pouring coffee while Mike cooked. Don guessed that much of the tidiness was his doing. Tubby pointed to the Coleman lamp. "Still the same mantles, Walter?"

"Sure," Walter said. "Of course they are. And the same generator. Five years this August and there's folks can't go a week without breaking them mantles."

Tubby laughed. "Must be a world's record. The Coleman people would pay you good money for it for advertising."

Both Mike and Walter sat down and drank coffee when the boys had finished eating. The gray cat was curled asleep on the back of an armchair. Tubby asked Walter, "Do you think the blueback run in the channel will last for a while?"

Walter looked across at the cat. "How long they been catching fish out there, Babe? 'Bout a week?" Babe opened one eye at the sound of his name, then closed it again.

Mike's deep voice said: "She'll likely be good for a few days yet, but they'll be hard to find soon as the tides get small again. Where you boys figuring to go from here?"

"North," Don said. "Up around Pendennis Island. There's always springs there and sometimes a good run of cohoes."

Mike nodded. "There's a lot of trollers go north now or out to the West Coast, and they're the boys that make her. But there's still money inside when prices are right."

Don and Tubby helped clean up the dishes, then went out to their bunks in the *Mallard*. As they undressed Don said: "Those are two swell old guys, but there's something wrong there. I've been trying all evening to figure what it is."

Tubby laughed. "You and me both. But I think I've got it doped out now. They ain't speaking."

Don looked up at him sharply. "Gee, Tubby, I believe you're right." He thought hard for a moment or two. "Yes, I'm darn sure you are. They spoke to us and they spoke to the cat, but they didn't say a word to each other all evening. Why do they call the cat Babe?"

"Paul Bunyan's blue ox. They both think the world of that darn cat; but I still don't get that angle, though. I never heard 'em talk to it like that when I was here before."

"I think I get it. When they're by themselves they've got to say things, so they say them to the cat and answer to the cat. That way the other guy gets the drift. And they've been at it so long it's got to be a habit, so they do it even when we're around." He began to laugh.

Tubby laughed with him, harder and harder until they were both almost helpless. "The old nuts," Tubby said at last. "They must've quarreled about something. 'Tain't so funny really." But he began to laugh again.

Don shook his head solemnly. "It's a heck of a note. We ought to do something about it, Tub."

"Sure we ought. But what?"

"I don't know," Don said. "We'll figure it out tomorrow."

They were out of the bay and fishing the eddy behind the island by first daylight the next morning. The tide was right and they began to catch fish almost at once, fishing shallower lines than they had the day before, but still working the eddy behind the island. As the tide changed the fishing slacked off, but they had a pile of fish under the forward hatch by that time. They both felt good, competent and sure of themselves. Don said, "We'd better have a mug-up while we hunt around to see if we can pick 'em up somewhere else."

It was a bright, warm day with a light breeze blowing down the channel from the east. They ate out on deck and Tubby said, "That breeze could bring up bad weather."

"Wouldn't hurt us any in here" Don said. "Say, Tubby, what are we going to do about Mike and Walter? We can't just leave 'em not speaking."

"What can we do?" Tubby asked. "They're a pair of obstinate old coots and I guess they know their own minds."

"There's got to be something. We could drown the cat. They'd have to talk then."

"They'd talk to the mulligan pot on the stove. And anyway, they're both crazy about Babe."

"What about the gas lamp?" Don said. "Knock it off the table and break those precious mantles. That might jar 'em into something."

Tubby gave the idea serious consideration as he bit into a bacon sandwich, but he shook his head at last. "Walter'd break your neck if you broke those mantles. And I'm not sure but what Mike'd think it was a good joke."

"I'd have Walter break 'em himself."

"Might be better" Tubby said. "But I don't see how you'd do it. We could try and get them into some kind of an argument where they'd forget and start talking."

They reached no very satisfying decision and Don kept worrying over it during the afternoon fishing. Three or four boats had come up the channel and were fishing through the eddy, but the fish were more scattered or else not feeding so freely, because neither the *Mallard* nor the newcomers caught much. Tubby said at last, "Let's work on up-channel and see what we find. It's kind of a break the fish aren't here, anyway. We should get the place to ourselves again tomorrow morning."

They passed two squat, snub-nosed purse seine boats with great nets piled on turntables at the stern. "Looking for humpbacks," Tubby said. "But they'll take anything they find if there's enough of it schooled together. Trollers are supposed to be against those guys, but Dad says that's crazy. All fishermen have got to work together."

"They say they waste a lot of young fish," Don said.

"Could be," Tubby agreed. "But don't ever think we don't waste fish too. There's plenty pull off the hooks and go away hurt pretty bad. Just the same," he added, "I wouldn't mind skippering one of those babies some day. I believe I could find fish with the best of 'em when I got on to it."

They worked a long way up the channel and had caught only a few more scattered fish when the buyer came up to them. But the morning tide had made it a good day and they felt satisfied when they turned to run back to Walter's Killarney Bay.

"Figured anything about how to get those guys to talking?" Tubby asked.

"Plenty," Don told him. "But I'm not sure any of it will work."

"Such as what?"

"Well, there's that cat. And the gas lamp. I know darn well a guy could work out something there. I've got to study out the place a bit tonight. Listen, Tub, can they both swim?"

Tubby thought for a moment. "No," he said. "I know Walter can't because he fell in once and nearly drowned. Mike had to save him, so he can. They told me that last year."

"That's a help," Don said. "What does Babe like to eat? Fish?"

"Won't touch it," Tubby said. "Eagle stew is about all he'll ever eat. That was it in the big pot on the stove last night. What's on your mind, Don? Spill it."

"I'm not sure yet. I've got to figure it out. I'll tell you soon as it seems to make sense. What do you figure they quarreled about?"

Tubby shrugged his shoulders. "Could be anything. They're both Irish, but Walter likes to remember it and Mike likes to forget it. Could be something of that. And they argue a whole lot about tides, get mad as heck sometimes. I don't think it'd be that though." He shook his head. "I wouldn't know. Not between those two."

7

They came into the bay earlier than they had the previous evening and again Mike was out in front of the shack. Walter came to the door as they were tying up the boat. "Supper's on, boys. Come right on in."

Don had been working on the engine as they were running in and he said: "Go ahead, Tubby, I've got to wash this grease off; then I'll be right with you."

Don had meant it to work out that way, so that he would have a moment or two to look around by himself. He was luckier than he had expected to be, because the big gray cat jumped aboard the *Mallard* instead of following Mike and Walter and Tubby as they turned into the shack. Don spoke softly to him. "Well, Babe, it's sure lucky you're a tomcat. A nice little lady cat would never have left her bosses like that."

Babe followed him confidently into the pilothouse. Don held out a hand and Babe lifted his head against the palm, rubbed his back along it, and jumped down from the pilothouse steps into the engine room. Don went through into the cabin, took a small can of chicken from the food locker, opened it, and dumped it on a plate. He put the plate on the floor and Babe came to it. He began to eat at once and Don heard him purr with satisfaction. "Chicken or eagle, it's all the same to you, old-timer," Don said. "Hope it doesn't make a sissy out of you so Mike'll notice."

While the cat was eating Don washed his hands. Then he went to one of the cabin portholes and watched the water carefully for about half a minute. Satisfied, he turned into the cabin and spoke to the cat again, pitching his voice in the flat tones he had noticed both Walter and Mike using when they spoke to Babe. "I think it's going to work, old Babe. That tide sets right away from the shore and along the boom for as far as I can see. It'll give you a good ride if I can get you afloat. And if you start from the stern of the boat you'll never come close enough to the boom to do any jumping." Babe looked up, licked his whiskers, squinted his eyes contemptuously, and went back to his eating. But Don felt he was getting somewhere. The chicken was disappearing fast and Babe seemed completely at home. He left the cat still eating and went up on deck. As he stepped from the *Mallard* to the float he confirmed what he had remembered from the previous evening—a small, cranky-looking dugout lay a little ahead of where the *Mallard* was tied, and just behind it was a small platform, about a foot square, spiked to a place on the boomstick that had been flattened off with an axe. The scuffing of Walter and Mike's spiked shoes led across the center of the platform, but Don noticed grease stains as well. "Eagle meat," he told himself as he went into the shack.

It was still light after supper and Don went out to the float. Babe was there and came up to rub against his legs. Mike came to the door and watched. "First time I ever seen him make up to a stranger that way," he said.

Don bent down and scratched Babe's ear. "Could be he smells old Tinker, our barn cat back home. I was wearing these pants when I was home." He didn't want to seem too much interested in Babe.

Mike went back into the cabin for a moment and came back with a handful of bones and cooked meat. Babe looked up at him and gave forth the high-pitched growl that served him in place of the plaintive mew of lesser cats. Mike walked to within a few feet of the platform on the boomstick and threw the meat onto it. Babe made a beautiful, unhesitating leap from the float to the platform across fully five feet of water, landing gracefully but heavily enough to roll the boomstick a little. He rode the corresponding movement of the platform with complete confidence. And Don began to feel that his plan really had a chance to work.

"There's a cat that is a cat," Mike said proudly. "Nearly ten years now since he first come up in the woods with us and he hasn't missed a working day yet. Seems like he gets as much kick out of seeing a tree come down or a log roll into the water as we do."

When they went back into the cabin, Walter was carefully lighting the gas lamp that he had just as carefully filled a few minutes before supper. The mantles burst into clear white light as he turned the valve and drew away the two halfburned matches with which he had heated the generator. He set the shade on the lamp and pushed it back to the center of the table with a sigh of satisfaction. "There's a light for ye. What folks wants with electrics is more than I kin see."

"Look, Walter," said Don. "Suppose you and Mike have supper with us on the boat tomorrow night. We figure to come in early and we'll cook you up a real meal."

Walter considered the matter slowly. "'Twould not be right," he said at last. "With you visitors to Killarney Bay an' all." He turned to the cat, who had just come into the cabin. "'Twould hardly be a right thing, Babe. What d'ye say?"

Don noticed that Mike had snorted again at the mention of Killarney Bay. It seemed to be a snort of indignation and disgust, but he spoke gently to the gray cat. "I don't rightly know about that, Babe. Folks likes to have company sometimes as much as they like to go visiting. There's pleasure in both ends of it. If Tubby and Don want to put up a meal for us, I'd be right proud to go aboard and eat with them."

Don was in great good spirits the next morning. The fishing on the early tide was good, though not as good as it had been the morning before, and they had the eddy to themselves. After the tide changed Don rigged larger spoons on the two deep lines. "May as well give the spring salmon a real chance," he told Tubby. "Unless we find a few today we'd better be on our way."

Tubby agreed. "Looks that way," he said. "Morning tide is only around seventeen feet tomorrow and there's nothing much over sixteen for a week after that."

They trolled carefully, working the places Tubby remembered from the previous season, but by noon they had caught only three small spring salmon at widely scattered intervals. Don went down into the cabin and came back on deck with a large, square butter box, a hammer, a hand axe, and some lead. He settled himself on a hatch cover and began to pound the lead into four long flat strips. Tubby watched curiously. "What's all that for?" he said at last. "Some new way to catch salmon?"

"It's my cat-boat," Don said. "The Blue Ox Special. I figure that if we put Babe in some spot that calls for quick action, Mike and Walter are liable to get excited enough to talk to each other. They'll have to. Babe won't be there to help out. And this," Don tapped the bottom of the box with his hammer, "is the spot."

"I still don't get it," Tubby said. "Go on." "You'll get it," Don told him. "Let me finish it. It'll make more sense then."

Don cut each of his lead strips down the center, so that it would fold, then clinched all four of them tightly to the four edges of the open end of the butter box. He passed the result to Tubby. "I want it to float bottom up, fairly steady, on even keel. How about it?"

Tubby examined the box carefully. It was waxed inside, airtight, well made, but not much over a foot square. "That's enough lead to hold it fairly steady. But you better find a way to let some air out if you want her to set down good."

Don fetched a brace and bit and drilled two holes in the side of the box. "Okay?" he asked. "Should be," Tubby said. "But it won't be so awful steady." "I'm not sure I want it to be," Don told him.

The fish buyer came down the channel early and the *Mallard* was tied up in Killarney Bay before Mike and Walter were back from their timber claim on the sidehill. Don had tied the boat so that she lay a little farther back than usual along the float, with her stern out of sight of the cabin windows. Tubby said: "They'll be back any time now. Go ahead and grab it. I'll get supper started."

Don opened the cabin door cautiously, feeling like a thief. The stove was out and he went across to it, took the lid off the big mulligan pot and picked out several choice pieces of Babe's favorite food. He crept out of the cabin, closed the door, glanced guiltily around, then jumped back aboard the *Mallard*.

"Gee," he told Tubby, "I wouldn't like to be in the burglary business. It feels awful to go into a man's place like that."

Tubby laughed. "I tried the box," he said. "Rides fine. I left it in the cockpit."

Five or ten minutes later Mike and Walter came down from the hill. They greeted the *Mallard* from the float and went into the cabin to clean up. Babe went in with them, but the door was open.

"Gosh!" Tubby said. "Suppose he doesn't come out again!"

But Babe remembered the canned chicken and came out. He stood for a long moment on the float while the boys watched from the cabin porthole, then walked along until he was opposite the forward hatch cover and made a smooth leap to the *Mallard*'s gunwale. Without hesitation he crossed the deck, entered the pilothouse, and came through to the cabin. He growled affectionately and rubbed himself against Don's leg.

"Okay, Tubby," Don said. "Do your stuff."

Tubby disappeared up on deck. Don picked up the meat he had taken from the cabin and showed it to Babe. Babe growled again, rubbed again, and stood his tail straight up. Don went up on deck, Babe following. Tubby was in the cockpit, holding the box bottomside up in the water, just outside the *Mallard*'s stern.

"How's the current?" Don asked.

"Setting just right," Tubby said.

Babe was walking the gunwale, almost directly above the box. "Here you are, Babe." Don said and threw the meat onto the box. Babe jumped immediately and landed neatly. Tubby held the box, steadying it. Babe grabbed a mouthful of meat, looked up at Tubby, laid his ears back and growled fiercely. Tubby let the box go. It tilted, Babe shift-ed his weight a little, and it rode almost evenly. Babe settled down to his meal, while the box drift-ed slowly away from the boat and Don and Tubby crept softly back down to the cabin.

"Gee," Tubby said, "what if it rolls over and he drowns."

Don was watching from a porthole. "He's doing fine so far. Anyway, cats can swim." But he felt a little scared.

Tubby glanced out of the porthole on the other side of the boat. "Walter's filling the lamp. They'll be along any minute."

"Swell!" Don said. "Listen, Tub, if you get a chance, break those mantles." He looked out of his own porthole again. The box was a hundred feet away, heading well out into the bay, and Babe was still feeding comfortably.

"Gosh," Tubby said, "here comes Mike."

They both watched as Mike stood in the doorway. "He wants to say something to Walter," Tubby said. "He's looking for Babe."

Mike looked up and down the float. He called: "Babe! Here, Babe! Where you got to?" Then he looked out and saw the box floating in the middle of the bay. "Babe!" he yelled in a voice that rattled the bells at the top of the *Mallard*'s forty-foot poles. "Hey, Walter! Come quick! Babe's out in the chuck" He turned and ran along the float, past the end of the cabin and out on to the boomstick

"Up we go," Don said and he and Tubby rushed up on deck just as Walter came out of the cabin. Don looked toward the boom. Mike was in the water, swimming. Walter ran out on the boomstick, waving his arms wildly. "Come back, Mike, ye old fool. Come back, man, ye'll drown sure."

Don slipped from the *Mallard*'s deck, ran along the float log, loosed the little dugout and jumped into it. He called to Mike. "Go back, Mike. I'll get Babe. Go on back" He saw Mike turn and sighed with relief. Kneeling in the stern he heeled the dugout far over to one side and drove the paddle with all the strength of his arms. Babe had looked up at Mike's wild shout, and for the first time had lost interest in the eagle meat. Babe became a badly scared cat. He moved, tilted the box, got his tail wet, scrambled forward, tilted it the other way, and almost went in head first. Don drove the dugout close, Babe crouched, sprang, landed neatly in the bow. Don looked around. Tubby and Walter were helping a bedraggled Mike back on to the boomstick, teetering dangerously themselves. Then Tubby went in with a splash and he and Mike were looking at each other across the log. Walter said: "He's got Babe. It's all right, Mike, he's got Babe."

Babe had entirely recovered his poise and was sitting calmly, high on the bow of the dugout.

Only his wet tail spoiled his dignity and even that seemed to bother him little enough. Tubby and Mike finally climbed back to the boomstick and all three met Don at the float as he came back with Babe and the dugout.

"The only sober man in the bunch of us," Mike said. "I plumb forgot about the dugout." He reached his big wet hands forward and rubbed Babe behind the ears. "Poor old Babe," he said. "Poor old Babe. Why did you want to do a fool thing like that?" Babe drew his head away and shook it. He was in no mood for more wetness. "Must've jumped on the box and then got panicky," Mike added.

"But it was sure a brave thing ye did, Mike, and I honor ye for it," Walter said.

"It was all our fault," Tubby said. "We should have known better than to throw that darn box overboard." Babe was on the float. He went to rub against Mike's legs, turned from the wetness, and rubbed against Walter's instead. The attention embarrassed Walter and he said: "Gee, Mike, the mantles got broke in my hurry."

Don figured this was the time. "First time I've heard you two talk together," he said.

They looked at each other sheepishly. Mike held out a hand. "Killarney Bay it is," he said.

Walter took the hand. "No," he said. "Canada Bay, the way you said."

"Killarney Bay it is, I said." Mike threw his big chest out.

"You and Tubby better get dry clothes," Don said hastily. "I'll be putting supper on."

As Tubby was changing his clothes, Don said, "You sure were quick with those mantles."

"I didn't break them," Tubby said. "He did."

"Boy, oh boy, what a neat little show that was," Don said. "Quiet," he added. "Here they come."

Mike and Walter came down into the cabin.

"Where's Babe?" Tubby asked.

"Won't come aboard. Guess he's had all the navigating he wants for a while."

When they were sitting down Mike said: "You boys got to settle an argument for us. Should a place like the bay here be called by an old country name or a new Canadian name?"

Tubby looked at Don. "I think Canadian."

"Like what?" asked Walter.

"Like—like Laurier. Or Buchan. Or McKenzie."

Walter snorted. "A Frenchman and two Scotsmen."

"Foreign names are okay if they stand for something Canadian," Don said. "Look at *Falaise* for Red's boat."

"*Falaise*? I remember the name. In the war news," Mike said.

"That's right. Where the Canadians closed the gap in Normandy. Red says he uses it because that's where he was wounded and got out of the war. But it isn't that really. You can tell he's proud of it."

"*Falaise*," Mike said softly. "It's a good sounding name for a boat and I remember about it now. It was a tough piece of fighting too. But what did Killarney ever do for Canada?"

Don smiled and looked across at Walter. "Sent us a lot of good Irishmen, I guess."

8

Don and Tubby pulled out of Killarney Bay early on the morning after the rescue of Babe and continued their journey north after taking on gas at Sullivan's camp. It was a good day, without wind, when they turned out of Viscount Channel and back into the main northward passage, but Tubby said: "We've had our share of good weather. I'm scared it's going to turn any time now."

Don had a lot of respect for Tubby's weather predictions on salt water, and they were coming now into water that neither of them knew. "Why do you think that?" he asked.

"There's not much reason, except there should be a bit of westerly coming down at us by this time of day if she's set for fine. And I don't know as I like the look of that sky, even though it is clear."

"Okay, what do you think we ought to do about it?"

"I don't believe we ought to figure on running right through. The Sound is a long stretch of open water for a small boat. We'll be crossing it in the dark if we run straight through."

Don felt lazy and comfortable. Normally he would have wanted to drive ahead, partly to get to the fishing grounds but more to answer the challenge to himself and his boat that running the Sound represented. But the stay in Viscount Channel had been successful and he was still feeling good about the solution of the Walter and Mike problem. "Fine," he said. "We'll take it easy and see how she looks tomorrow. The way the tides are we've got eight hours' running anyway before we come to real open water. We can hole up somewhere for the night and go on tomorrow morning."

Tubby was used to Don's impatience with overcaution and the hard recklessness that usually controlled his decisions. The ready agreement surprised him. "I know it's early to start fretting," he said, using the words he had expected from Don. "And I might be crazy about the weather. But it could be miserable out there in the dark, running on just a compass, if it came up to blow."

"We're rich—over a hundred and fifty bucks in the till. We don't have to hurry and it's a peach of a day so far."

After a little while, Don said: "I wish we were tied up alongside the old *Falaise*. I miss that Red guy. One thing about this fishing, you sure get around and meet people."

"We'll likely find someone else to tie alongside of before we get to Pendennis Island. But I think I'd as soon cross the Sound on our own."

"If that southeaster of yours comes up," Don agreed. "Wonder what Mike and Walter are doing now."

"Up on their claim cutting down trees and talking a blue streak at each other. Do you think the cure'll last?"

"Sure I do. They were both looking for an easy way out of it when we arrived there. They won't pull that again, but I don't say they won't think up something else just as crazy. In the winter I guess they're lucky if they see another human being once in a month."

"They lay in three months' grub on the first of October, then another three months' on the first of January, so they won't have to go out between times. They told me that."

The Strait was full of purse seine boats, some cruising in search of fish, some making sets, some brailing fish from their pursed nets. Don and Tubby recognized some of the boats from down on the Gulf, but most were strange.

"Must be the run of humps they were talking about at Sullivan's," Don said. "You'd wonder where all the boats come from at ten or twenty thousand bucks a throw."

A big boat was plowing up abeam of them, two or three hundred yards nearer shore. Her skipper was at the wheel on his flying bridge on the roof of the pilothouse, watching the water ahead and to either side. Suddenly the heavy white wave dropped away from her bow and she began to slow.

"He's seen fish bubbles or something," Tubby said. "He's going to set." Don slowed the *Mallard*. "May as well watch. I've never seen a purse seine set close to."

The crew of the purse seiner was out on deck. Her diesel speeded again, briefly, and the skipper swung his boat toward the shore a little more. Two men jumped onto the pile of net at the stern and slid a heavy skiff from it into the water. One jumped into the skiff and picked up the oars. He began to row, pulling away from the big boat, and the net began to tumble over the stern roller into the water as the skiff held the end of it. The big boat began to circle and they could see the line of corks that floated the net on the water behind it. The net flowed out smoothly, lead line and web hissing into the water, as the crew paid it out over the stern roller.

"Smooth operators," Tubby said. "That's an Alert Bay boat. It takes organization to put out a quarter of a mile of net quick and easy like that."

The big boat completed her circle back to the skiff and the skiffman stood up and passed his rope back to the deck. The crew went to work fast, bringing the ropes in over the capstans of the power winch on deck and piling the slack of the net back on the turntable at the stern. Very quickly the circle of corks was narrowed to a diameter of only fifty or sixty feet, on the starboard side of the boat. Don was holding the *Mallard* in close, and they could see fish turning and swirling and milling as the purse line brought the web up underneath them and forced them to the surface. Corks bobbed as fish drove into the web and tried to escape, but the circle drew in until it was only a narrow space between the skiff and the boat. An occasional fish splashed, here and there a dorsal fin showed above water or a tail fin flopped over, but the fish were surprisingly quiet.

Tubby said, "Looks like a pretty good set." He went out on deck and shouted across to one of the purse seine crew. Don heard the man's voice across the quiet water, excited and cheerful. "Sockeyes," he shouted. "Close to a thousand, looks like. Better get yourselves a net."

"We'll make out," Tubby shouted back.

The purse seiner lowered the big dip net from her mast, swung it out over the closed net, and lowered it. One of her crew grabbed the handle and dipped it full of fish. The block and tackle raised the brail again, swung it back over an open hatch. Someone tripped the net and a silver shower of sockeye salmon tumbled into the hold. The brailing went on, dip net after dip net full of fish, until at last Don reached for the throttle, speeded up, and swung the *Mallard* back on course again.

"A neat thousand bucks in one haul," he said. "Not bad."

"They work for it," Tubby said. "Lots of times they make a set for half a dozen humpbacks or nothing at all. Still, a good skipper with a good boat and a good crew can really make her that way."

Through the rest of the day they worked lazily on up the Strait, turning off course occasionally for a closer look at the shore line of an island, to pass near a school of blackfish, or to settle some argument about a passing boat or a scow or log boom in tow. It was a pleasant day, quiet but with a strong sense of adventure in new water. And there was not a stirring of breeze up or down the Strait all through the long afternoon.

It was well on in the afternoon when Tubby said: "Where'll we tie up tonight? We could make Blunden Harbor in lots of time."

Don hesitated. He was tired of the pounding of the *Mallard*'s engine, tired of the still day and the miles upon miles of salt water that confined them to the few feet of space on the deck and in the pilot-house and cabin. For some reason he did not want to go into one more fishing harbor, to tie among fishing boats, to talk fishing boats and smell fish. "I don't know, Tub," he said. "I'd as soon sneak in some bay or other on our own. We don't need gas or anything."

"Okay," said Tubby. "Where?"

Don pulled down a chart he had been study-ing earlier and pointed to a tight narrow bay on the mainland coast north of Blunden Harbor. "How about that? Looks like a lagoon in back of it."

"Seems like lots of shelter, even without the lagoon." Tubby felt disappointed. It would have been good to go into Blunden Harbor and see what boats were in there, maybe find someone you knew and talk about the weather and the fishing. But at the same time he was beginning to know Don better than Don knew himself, and he realized that Don was very close to one of the irritable, depressed, even quarrelsome moods that he often worked himself into when he had a decision to make. "It looks like a pretty good place," Tubby said. "But if we went into the Harbor we might get some weather dope."

"The heck with that," Don said. "I wouldn't want to wait around any longer than tonight. In daylight the old *Mallard*'ll take anything the Sound can throw up. I'd like to go ashore though and take a look around if that bay is a halfway decent place."

It was early evening, with several hours of daylight still left, when they turned into Don's bay. It was narrow, twisting, tight, more channel than bay, with rocky shores and scrub timber. Don eased the *Mallard* slowly at the center of it, watching for rocks, though the water seemed deep. They rounded a point and the bay widened into a sort of pocket. At the head of it was a beach and the narrow entrance to the lagoon. Tubby went up and stood on the bow. He signaled Don to turn to starboard and they passed within a few feet of a big rock that was almost out of water. Don slowed the motor still more when he saw it. "Think there's water enough to let us into the lagoon?" he asked Tubby. Tubby shook his head. Don kicked the clutch out. "Let's drop the hook right here then."

When the engine died it was dead still in the bay. Don went out on deck and looked around. "Gee," he said. "Sure is swell to be quiet for a change."

Tubby could feel something of what he meant. The silence was resting them. The evening light on the still water, on the gray rocks and dark green woods, took the strain of the sun's hard, day-long reflection away from their eyes. But he knew that Don was feeling more than this. Tubby was glad to be in a safe harbor at the end of a good day's run; he was happy in the smell of salt water about him and in the gleam of wet rocks and seaweed where the tide had drawn down on the beaches; he was curious about nothing beyond the high tide mark. But Don, Tubby knew, was looking beyond the line of driftwood that marked the tide's limit and wondering about the woods and hills that climbed away from the shore. He was not surprised when Don said, "Let's take the dinghy and go up into the lagoon."

So they launched the *Mallard*'s little dinghy from the top of the cabin and rowed up over the shallows into the lagoon. They were in a different world at once. The shores of the lagoon were sandy and reeds grew along the edge. There were ducks on the water—mergansers for the most part, but Don noticed a bright group of male harlequins. He rowed quietly and none of the ducks flew. "I bet there's geese here in the fall," he told Tubby. "And plenty of mallard and teal and canvasbacks too, likely. It's a swell place."

"Ought to be a creek coming in somewhere," Tubby said. He was beginning to feel a little of Don's enthusiasm and sense of exploration. "Wonder no one's ever settled in here."

They found the creek, a wide flow of clear water over a rocky beach, and near it an old cabin rotting back into the moss and dampness of the forest. "Trapper likely," Don said. "Nothing around here for a handlogger."

Tubby had gone a little way up the creek and was looking down into a deep pool below a log jam. He pointed down into it as Don came up. Four big trout were lying quietly where the pool began to shallow.

"Cutthroats," Tubby said. "Honeys, too. I should have brought my rod."

Then they saw two much larger fish, side by side in the deeper water. "What would those be?" Don asked. "Too early for salmon, surely."

"Steelheads, I guess," Tubby said slowly. "Spawned out and going back to the salt chuck. Must be."

Two or three more cutthroats circled back from the deep water of the pool and showed themselves on the shallows. They were very big fish, widebacked and long. "Holy smoke!" Don said. "We could stay over tomorrow morning and catch some of those babies." Then he checked himself.

"No," he said. "We've got to get out of here and make a dollar. We won't do it catching cutthroats."

Tubby was the keener and better trout fisherman of the two and Don was half hoping that he would want to stay. Tubby looked again at the broad backs of the cutthroats, imagined them turning to his flies and the thrill of setting the hook and feeling them run for the log jam. But he said: "I guess you're right, Don. We'd better keep moving."

9

It was blowing the next day. In the bay where they were anchored everything was quiet, but gray clouds were moving up overhead and they could hear the roar of the surf on the rocks outside.

"We come all this way in good weather," Don said, "then have to hit it like this for the Sound." He and Tubby were standing out on deck and he looked up at the gray sky. "Just a summer south-easter, though. Nothing we can't take. And there's no sense to waiting it out. It's liable to last a week after the fine spell we've had." He spoke confidently, but he was worried about Tubby's verdict.

"It isn't bad yet," Tubby said slowly. He was thinking: if it hadn't been for me, Don would have hit right on through last night and we'd made it into Fitzhugh Sound before this came up. "I think we can get across before it gets real tough if we start right out."

"Swell," Don said. "We'll check everything good and give her a whirl."

They made the *Mallard* snug in every possible way. Don worked on deck, tying down the anchor and the dinghy, fixing tight canvas over the hatch covers, checking the steering gear and the rigging of the small leg-of-mutton sail on the mast, securing anything and everything that could possibly move. Now that he was faced with making the run in a storm he was no longer worrying. Just for a moment he had wished the decision could have been clear-cut, ready-made, by a fine day or a really bad day. If anything went wrong after starting on a day like this, people would be able to say: "Those fool kids. They had no business off by themselves like that." But that was an old fear that he had faced often before and he was able to put it away from him easily. He had decided that the day was good enough for the run and the *Mallard* was good enough for both. His only worry now was the legitimate and practical one of making sure that everything was in shape to give the boat and themselves a fair chance.

He went below and found Tubby completing his check of the engine. "Seems perfect," Tubby said. "I've had the plugs out and been over all the lines. We've got lots of gas and we know the tank's clean. How's everything up above?"

"Jake," Don said. "Should take the sea anchor up where we can get at it, I guess. But that's all."

They went into the cabin, stowed away anything that could move, and checked the portholes. Tubby looked at the radio on its shelf. "That safe there?"

"Should take her down, I guess, even though she don't work. We might get her fixed some time. The batteries are still good. They're up under the bow."

It was strange to start out in flat calm, knowing what was waiting for them within half a mile of running. Don had the wheel, but Tubby was in the pilothouse making a last check of the compass course he had laid out on the chart. They came in sight of the entrance to the bay. There were whitecaps outside and a short swell. Don held for the southerly point, to give himself plenty of room to square away on the northwestward course before they came into the worst of it.

"How does she look?" he asked. "Fair enough," Tubby said. "Don't see spray flying off the whitecaps, so it's not a real blow yet."

The *Mallard* lifted to the first swells in the still smooth water, then they were past the point and Don felt the wind on her bow. The third swell in the open broke over the bow and splattered against the pilothouse windows.

"That's okay," Tubby said. "Soon as we get on course we'll be quartering them and we shouldn't take another one over all the way up."

The *Mallard* rolled her exhaust pipe under and the explosions of her two cylinders thudded into the water before she rolled back, but Don felt proud of the way she rode the cross swell and Tubby's quiet eyes were bright with excitement. "She really is a sea boat," he said. "Look at the way that bow lifts to 'em."

"We've been out in worse weather than this on the Gulf," Don said. "She's never pounded on me yet. She's a dry boat going into 'em and she's always kept her stern ahead of 'em going away. You can't ask much more."

They were well clear of the point now. Tubby said: "You can bring her up a little. We'll be running about ten degrees north of west when we come on course and I figure that ought to keep us quartering so long as this wind holds."

Don glanced at the chart. "Takes us a long way out, but I guess that's all to the good."

"You're darn right," Tubby said. "One thing I don't want to be is close to shore if anything goes wrong in this kind of weather."

The first hour of the run passed quickly. As soon as they had swung enough to put the wind well astern Tubby had broken out the leg-of-mutton sail. The *Mallard* heeled to it a little, steadied herself, then seemed to catch the rhythm of the swells and rode them like her namesake. Once something broke loose in the cabin and Tubby went down to secure it. When he came back Don gave him the wheel and went out on deck to tighten the rigging that held one of the trolling poles to the mast.

By the end of the first hour they knew that the wind had freshened a lot. It was picking spray from every whitecap and scudding it across the water in a low mist all around them. The sky was darker too, and it had begun to rain. The smooth backs of the swells, behind their crests, were veined with white, and hissing. Don still felt the excitement of the storm, but he remembered they had three more hours of running ahead of them before they came to sheltered water again. "It's fine so far, Tub," he said. "But it's just about enough."

"You're darn right." Tubby steadied himself against a sharper roll than usual, glanced quickly astern and back at the compass. As he did so the exhaust pipe buried itself again, rolled clear, buried itself. "There's a change in that wind," Tubby said. "It's a whole lot nearer due south than it was." He glanced at the compass again. "No, by golly, it's west of south." He eased the *Mallard*'s bow over until she was heading only ten or fifteen degrees west of north by the compass, but the swells were bigger now and the *Mallard* still rolled well over from time to time in spite of the steadying sail and the quartering sea. "Straight from the open Pacific," said Tubby a little grimly.

They both laughed, and as they did there was a sharp change in the sound of the engine. "Take her," Tubby said quickly and disappeared below. He was back almost at once. "Cracked exhaust pipe," he said.

"Wrap something around it," Don said, then he looked at Tubby and saw he was worried.

"Can't. It's back in the manifold."

Don whistled. "Can we fix it at all?"

"Not and keep running."

"Could we run anyway?"

"Not safe," Tubby said.

"Okay. Head up into it under power, then cut?"

Tubby nodded. "Put out the sea anchor and the sail will help some to hold her head into it. Shouldn't be bad. I'll go and get the tools out."

Don began to swing the *Mallard*. She came into the trough and rolled until his feet slipped on the pilothouse floor and he thought she never would come back. As she righted herself a crest smashed into her port side and there was solid green water against the pilothouse windows. Something crashed below with the hit of the wave. The engine choked, hesitated, picked up, and plugged on. Don saw Tubby's face, wet and pale, with blood on it, looking up at him. He forced the wheel hard over and the *Mallard* took green water again. The motor choked again and died.

Tubby was up in the pilothouse. "Doused," he said. "But she's coming into it. Get that sea anchor out while she's still got steerage way. I'll hold her."

Don went on deck. As he clambered round the pilothouse the *Mallard* took another sea that soaked him and almost tore his hands away from the rail. He found the sea anchor, tossed it over, and held the line until he felt the pull of it. Twice more, while he paid out the full length of line, water broke over him, but it no longer had the same fierce weight behind it and he knew the *Mallard* was riding well.

As he came back into the pilothouse Tubby said, "Nice going."

Don saw that the blood on his face was from a cut on the forehead. "What's the damage?" he asked.

"Plenty. That first sea broke the window above the engine. The second one doused everything. We'll be lucky if we get started again."

They both went below. Tubby began to work with a wrench on the bolts that held the hot manifold. An inch or more of water was slopping greasily over the engine-room floor with each roll of the boat. "Dry her off all you can," Tubby said. "Plugs, wires, batteries, the whole darn ignition system."

For the next half hour they worked steadily. Occasionally Don went up into the pilothouse to check things on deck, but the *Mallard* was riding the big swells beautifully and her high bow seemed to shake the water away from itself each time it rose. Don felt an emptiness in his stomach that he knew was fear, and neither he nor Tubby talked very much. When they did, their voices were strained and tense. Tubby said at last, "I believe it'll hold." He had been working without a break, cutting strips of tin, drilling holes, molding asbestos packing, fitting and testing and fitting again. The manifold was back in place, Don had pumped the bilge until it was almost dry and had gone outside to nail a board over the shattered window.

"Now," Tubby said, "if she'll only start."

They took the plugs out of the oven of the little stove and screwed them back in place, hooked the batteries up again, rechecked the timer. Tubby primed the carburetor, set the johnson bar in the fly wheel, and turned her over. There was no sign of life. He adjusted the choke, swung again, and the engine was still dead.

Tubby shook his head. "Batteries, I'm afraid," he said. But he tried again half a dozen times while Don tried to get a spark from the plugs. A heavy sea smashed against the *Mallard*'s bow, sending a shock right through her. For the first time since he had gone forward to put out the sea anchor, Don felt helpless. He looked into Tubby's white, sweating face, still smeared with blood, and smiled, not too cheerfully.

"'Tain't funny," Tubby said. "That wind'll put us on the beach if we don't get running. And if it comes up much more it won't have to put us on the beach."

"And if we do get running, we've got to get turned round again. What'll we do? Dry out that darn battery some more?"

Tubby went up into the pilothouse and looked out at the rough water. Don began to un-hook the battery again. Suddenly Tubby was back beside him. "We're in sight of land," he said. "And that's too darn close in this muck."

"How long?" Don asked.

"Half an hour maybe. You go up and hold off all you can with that sail. I'll shove the battery in the oven and burn out those plugs again."

Don went up into the pilothouse and swung the wheel over. He saw the *Mallard*'s bow swing out sluggishly, but he knew it would do little to counter-act the drift. The land was in plain sight abeam on the port side and he saw the dim outline of a long point astern. "That sure ties it up," he told himself. "It's more like fifteen minutes than half an hour."

He heard Tubby swing the fly wheel. Tubby swung again, both cylinders fired, missed, fired again, and caught. Tubby was up in the pilothouse with him. "Those radio batteries," he said. "I'd forgotten about them."

Don held out his hand and they shook on it and laughed. "She's yours," Don said. "Creep her ahead while I get that sea anchor in."

10

They came to Pendennis Island late on the evening of the third day after leaving Viscount Channel. Once they were safely across the Sound they had followed inside channels all the way up. The continuing southeast wind had been a help to them, in spite of a few short stretches where choppy seas, sharply broken by the fierce meeting of tide and wind, had battered at the *Mallard* and tossed her about more than had the big swells of the Sound.

The cannery settlement was in Hardnose Cove, on the inside of the island. Tubby said, "They built new floats in there last year and nearly all the small boats tie up there nights."

They passed several boats with lines out as they came up Hughes Channel, and more off Sad Point, the southerly tip of the island. But when they turned into the Cove it seemed full of boats of every size and shape, gill netters and a few seine boats, as well as trollers. Don knew he had been hoping for something like this, something that seemed as though fishing were serious business and not just a casual, rather haphazard way of earning a living. He slowed the *Mallard* right down so that they could pick a place to tie up and at the same time get a good look at the harbor. Both he and Tubby began to recognize boats almost at once. "There's Johnny Eliot's *Wanderer*," Tubby said. "And Gerry Temple's *Rita*. There's the *Otter* and the *Marlin*. Boy, everybody's here."

"And Phil Eastey's *Kingfisher*," Don added. Phil Eastey was the man from whom he had bought the *Mallard*. "And there's Happy Jackson's *Summer Duck* and Happy's aboard too. Let's go tie alongside him."

So they edged in alongside the little gray *Summer Duck*. Happy was sitting on deck, a bucket of water between his knees, a week or more of laundry accumulating on the line that slanted down behind him from the mast to the stern. He looked up only when Tubby spoke to him. "Well, well, look who's here." He stood up and held out a wet and soapy hand. "Red in the *Falaise* said you was coming but I wasn't looking for you for a few days yet, with this weather."

Happy was a lot like his boat, little and gray and tidy, serviceable but getting on in years. He was a year-round troller who moved from place to place following the runs all summer, then holed up in some favorite harbor during the winter to go out in search of spring salmon whenever the weather was good enough.

"How long has Red been in?" Don asked.

"Four or five days, I guess," Happy said. "Been high boat ever since he come."

"How is it? Don't say it's lousy. They tell us that every place."

Happy grinned. "It ain't awful good. But you know me. I never was one to bust a gut looking for fish, and the weather's been hard enough to keep 'most everybody around the harbor the last little while. Red and some of the other big boats have been going outside, weather or no, and Red's brought in two or three real catches, big springs mostly."

"How about the others?"

"They've had fish, but not the way Red has. He says he's fishing real deep-fifty fathom and over."

"Steel lines and gurdey spools," Don said. "That's too deep for us."

They talked on about the fishing and boats and fishermen. The *Falaise* was out. She had left that morning and Happy thought she'd stay out overnight. "There's plenty of others you know here. Phil Eastey is in and Jerry Temple," Happy said. "And there's a lot of young fellows. You'd better go on up and get acquainted. They're usually collected up around somebody's boat by this time of night."

Don and Tubby walked along the planks of the long float and Tubby said: "Kind of a good feeling, coming in and finding guys you know. Fishermen are an awful good bunch mostly."

"That Happy," Don said, "I've never seen him different. Always cheerful and glad to see you, yet he keeps to himself, somehow."

"Happy catches fish. He don't seem to work at it, but it isn't often he doesn't do all right. I've got a lot of respect for Happy. There's plenty of guys think they can go out or stay in when they choose, the way he seems to, and still make her pay. But they can't."

"I hadn't thought of it like that," Don said. "But I guess you're right. What's the difference?"

"When Happy stays in or goes out, he's got some idea. When they stay in, it's just because they don't want to go out."

They came to the *Kingfisher* and saw Phil Eastey and half a dozen others aboard her. "Hello, Don," Phil said. "I knew that was the *Mallard* I heard come in just now, but I didn't see you. How's the boy?"

"Swell," Don said. "How's fishing?"

"No better'n fair. How's it down below?"

"We made money on bluebacks for a couple of days in Viscount Channel," Tubby said. "Then she kind of petered out."

"When did you cross the Sound?"

"Yesterday," Tubby said, and tried to make it sound casual.

Phil looked at them solemnly. "That *Mallard*'s a good little sea boat," he said. "But you want to remember she's not the *Lizzy*." He threw his cigarette butt into the water. "What you standing down there for, anyway? Better come aboard and meet some of the boys."

The next morning was calm and Don and Tubby pulled out of the Cove while it was still dark. They rounded Sad Point as the first light showed in the eastern sky and turned up along the outside of the island. There was a smooth, heavy swell on the open water and the sounds and lights of other boats were all about them. Some, they knew from the throttled-down engines, were already trolling.

"Where'll we try?" Don asked.

Tubby laughed. "Your guess is as good as mine," he said. "But the sun will be up in a few minutes and we'll get some sort of an idea from watching the other boats."

Don slowed the engine and watched the

light growing in the eastern sky. It was pearl gray at first and the tall peaks of the coast range stood blackly against it. Then there was a red flush and the same redness was in the long slow swells that lifted the *Mallard*. He took a deep breath of the cold air and knew that this was a large part of what he had come for. These were the fishing grounds that he had heard about and thought about for years. The *Mallard* was the boat he had longed for as something beyond attainment only a season ago. And he was with her and on equal terms among men who had seemed infinitely older and wiser and braver than himself a few months earlier. He looked at Tubby. "This is the life, boy," he said. "We're going to make a clean-up."

Tubby grinned. "Okay. We better get started then." He went out on deck and let the long poles down from the mast.

They had decided to fish as deep as their gear would let them, with only two big spoons to each line. Don came out on deck and helped Tubby put out the lines. The sun was up now and they found they were fishing about a mile from the shore of Pendennis Island. A few islets lay between them and the main island and there were others farther out. A dozen or more boats were fishing near them, passing and re-passing along what seemed a well defined line. Don said: "Take her a while, Tubby. I'll go down and check the stove and start breakfast."

When he came back on deck, Tubby had just brought in two small spring salmon on one of the lines.

"Starboard bow pole's loaded too," Tubby said.

Don pulled it and brought in two more fish about the same size. For the next half hour they pulled fish almost steadily; then the take slacked off. The sun grew hot and a light westerly breeze came in along the top of the big swells. The boats continued their slow rolling way, exhausts puffing steam, long poles spread like wings, bows dipping and lifting in easy motion. For a while they all held to roughly the same patrol, a mile or so northward, a wide circle, the southward mile and another long circle to bring them on the northward beat again. They were fishing a tidal eddy behind a sand bar, but few of the fishermen knew it because both bar and eddy were deep down under fathoms of salt water. Phil Eastey in the *Kingfisher* knew it, and because he knew it and knew what he was doing he was the first to turn away when the fish stopped taking. Don asked Tubby, "Where's he going?"

Tubby watched the big boat's already distant hull. "Search me," he said. "They were all talking last night about Hideaway Rocks. According to the chart they're somewhere up in the direction he's heading. It's getting on for slack tide, too. He must figure this place is only good on flood."

"He was catching fish after they quit taking us, too."

"Steel lines," Tubby said. "He likely went down deeper as the light got stronger. Most of the boats with steel lines caught fish after we quit."

Tubby went forward to the pilothouse and came out again with a chart in his hands. He spread the chart on the deck in front of the cockpit and they both leaned over it. Tubby pointed to a sixty fathom sounding almost due west of Sad Point. "That's about where we are now." His finger traced a few inches northwestward along the shore of Pendennis Island. "There's Hideaway Rocks. Around four miles from here. They don't show, even on the lowest tides, and it drops off pretty sharply all around 'em."

Don had looked at that part of the chart many times before, but now he saw it clearly for the first time. Pendennis was a biggish island, nearly thirty miles long and lying roughly northwestward and southeastward. It was separated from Butcher Inlet and Whale River on the mainland by Hughes Channel, up which they had come to reach Hardnose Cove. Passing Sad Point in the morning they had come through Wreck Pass. The western coast of the island, off which they were fishing, was broken by several bays and the chart showed shoal and rocky water at a dozen places along it.

"Gee," Don said. "It sure is a lot of water. A guy tells you he's been catching fish off Pendennis Island and it could mean anywhere in thirty miles north and south and anywhere in sixty miles east and west. Most everybody seems to have a different idea of where to go, at that."

Tubby pointed to a group of shallow soundings about ten miles westward of the island. "That's what they call the Big Bank," he said. "A lot of them go out there. Heck, we'll get on to it in time. We may even find good spots of our own, like the island in Viscount Channel. 'Most any place that makes an eddy is a fair bet."

Don looked around him at the other boats. They were more scattered than they had been, but nearly all had moved northward. The *Kingfisher* was well to the north, almost to Hideaway Rocks, he judged from the chart. "What do you say we look around a bit?" he asked Tubby. "We've got enough fish in the hold to buy a couple of days' grub and we might learn something that way."

"Okay by me. Where'll we go?"

Don pointed beyond Hideaway Rocks to the Sudden Point, a long spit of land that ran out from the island between Haida Bay and Sully Bay. "That looks like fish to me," he said. "And there's a good piece of shoal water around there, by the soundings."

11

It took them a full hour to make Sudden Point and they found plenty of boats there when they arrived. The Summer Duck was there and several of the larger boats that packed ice and stayed out for two or three days at a time. And there were boats of about the *Mallard*'s own size, most of them rigged better than she was, with gurdey spools and steel lines, and probably two to four feet longer, but still something less than real outside trollers. Don saw Hal Stevens' *Milltail*, Johnny Smith's *Jamaica*, Dave Swanson's *Varga Girl*. These were the "young fellows" Happy had spoken of, most of whom they had met aboard the *Kingfisher* the previous evening.

"Looks like we're in good company," Don said. "They're pulling fish, too." Tubby looked the place over and liked it. A foamy line of tide rip streaked southward to them from the point. The westerly breeze was fresher here and the big swell of the previous day's southeaster seemed to be dying away.

"Looks like you had yourself a smart hunch," he told Don and slowed the engine back to trolling speed. "This is our kind of place."

They put out the big spring salmon spoons again, fishing them at fourteen fathoms on the bow poles and a little more on the other lines. "Should be okay for a start," Don said. "The chart shows twenty and thirty fathom soundings all around here."

"May not be deep enough," Tubby said, "but we'll try it. If we do hit a good spell there won't be so darn much line to pull for every fish."

The bell on the tip of the starboard pole jingled sharply as he spoke and kept jingling. Don reached for the line and began to pull it in. "Gee," he said. "Something really powerful this time." He brought in three or four fathoms of line by working hard, held it there for a few moments, then had to let it run out again as the fish ran.

"Let him drag a couple of minutes," Tubby said. "That'll slow him down some." One of the other lines hooked a fish and he reached for that. "Boy," he said, "we're into big stuff! This baby packs some authority too."

Don began to get back line again and managed to keep his fish coming until it broke water fifty or sixty feet behind the boat. It fought there on the surface for several moments in a flurry of spray.

"Don't tear the hook out of him," Tubby said. He was working on his own fish which had swum up toward the boat and was still deep down in the water. Don's fish went down a little, then came out in a great clean jump. "Gosh!" Tubby said. "Must be fifty pounds, easy." The fish was strong for a little longer, then came in almost easily, on his side. Don picked up the claw hammer that was ready beside him, gave the fish a smart tap at the base of the skull, slipped the claw into his gills, and swung him into the cockpit in a single smooth motion. He freed the hook quickly, threw the spoon back in, and let the line out again. As the last lead went overboard Tubby lifted his fish in. They were a perfect pair, deep-bodied, hog-backed, cleanly gray and silver, the biggest pair of fish Don had ever seen.

"A hundred pounds of spring salmon right there," Tubby said. "Just like that. Let's go get some more."

Hal Stevens passed close to them, the six cylinders of the *Milltail*'s high-speed motor running smoothly at trolling speed. "How're you doing?" he shouted.

"Okay," Don said. "How long has it been like this?"

"Run of big springs," Stevens said. "Just in, I guess. They weren't here yesterday." Then the boats were beyond shouting distance.

For the next two or three hours most of the boats seemed to be catching fish fairly steadily, and Don and Tubby had their share. Toward five o'clock the westerly breeze began to die down and for the next hour or so they saw very few fish caught. The *Mallard*'s own lines cut the water smoothly and there was only one sharp jingle from one of her bells when a fish struck and was not hooked. Don noticed that the boats had begun to scatter again, most of them trolling their way slowly southward along the shore of the island. One or two took in their lines, raised their poles, and pulled right out. The *Milltail* came close again and Hal Stevens shouted, "Had enough?"

"It's kind of quiet," Don shouted back.

"Better pack up and start home," Hal said. "It's all over for today."

Don looked at Tubby and Tubby said, "I don't see why it couldn't pick up again later."

Don hesitated for a moment. He wanted to go on fishing, but he felt that they would be doing so blindly. After all, Hal had been at the island for some while and should know something. There might be more to be learned from talking with him than by hunting fish for another hour or two. "I don't know, Tub," he said at last. "We've got our share. It's away the best catch we've had all season. May as well run in with him."

So both boats took in their lines, Tubby eased the *Mallard* alongside the *Milltail*, and Don took his bow line aboard her. Hal was fishing alone. "No sense to burning gas for nothing," he said as Don came back to his pilothouse. "The late fishing's been lousy out here all season; nobody seems to know why. Most of the boys quit about this time. We'll pick up Johnny Smith and Dave Swanson farther down and we can all run in together."

They saw Johnny Smith take up his poles as they came down toward him. The *Jamaica* had a lot of power and Johnny used it freely. The *Mallard* and the *Milltail* were slowed to let him come alongside and he ran hard for the *Milltail's* port bow, kicked his clutch out, and went full astern at the last possible moment. The *Jamaica* threw out a foam of white water astern, swung broadside to the other two boats, and suddenly was running gunwale to gunwale, speed for speed with them. Johnny's partner, Dick Evans, came aboard and made the lines fast. Johnny's brown face and flashing white teeth grinned at them from the pilothouse and Hal said:

"I wish you wouldn't do that, Johnny. Scares the daylights out of me."

Johnny came out and stood easily on the deck, rolling a cigarette. He was tall and well built, with black curly hair, quick brown eyes, and a smiling, good-natured mouth. His shirt was open halfway down his brown chest and his thigh boots were turned down to his knees. "Don't be an old woman, Hal," he said. "The Jamaica's bound to feel her oats a bit after fifteen hours of trolling speed."

"One day that darn clutch'll give out on you," Hal said. "And somebody'll get hurt."

Dick Evans came aft. He was short, very heavily built, and stoop-shouldered, with black hair, black eyes, and thick black eyebrows that made a straight, unbroken line across his face.

"No use riding Johnny," he told Hal. "The guy was born crazy and he's going to stay that way." He turned to Don and Tubby. "How'd you make out? You'll never have it better than today."

"The boys got their share," Hal said. "What you got in there, Don?" He pointed to the *Mallard*'s hatch cover. "Hundred bucks or so?"

"Close to, I guess," Don said. "We had eight or ten real heavy fish this afternoon and some smaller ones besides."

A few minutes later Dave Swanson came up with his *Varga Girl* and tied outside the *Mallard*. "Who's got the beer?" he asked as he came aboard.

"'Bout time you had it," Dick Evans told him. "But we've got it, as usual. On ice too."

They had all collected aboard the *Milltail*, because she was the largest of the four boats. The conversation went away from Don and Tubby, left them accepted but only on the edge of things, because the others had traveled together a long time and seemed close friends. It was kidding, boasting fisherman's talk, jumping from boats to rigging to fish and weather, back to boats, away to girls and good times in town, memories of other seasons, other trolling grounds, other fishermen. Tubby listened contentedly enough, holding an open bottle of beer in his hand, drinking from it only occasionally because he didn't care much for it and knew he didn't. Tubby was used to listening a lot and talking little and the day had made him happy. Don was more impatient. He, too, was satisfied with the day, but he wanted to talk. Everything was exciting and good, a fulfillment of something he had been searching for. He wanted to be with these men and of them. The bottle of beer in his hand was the first that had ever been given him, and he watched how the others drank and drank with them. He waited his time to talk because he did not want to say anything foolish, but was not content to stay out on the edge of things.

Hal Stevens said: "Everybody was catching fish today. Looks like it's going to last for a spell."

"Don't look that way to me," Dick Evans said. "Those big babies are traveling by this time of year, heading for home somewhere in the south. They'll be in for a day or two, then on their way somewheres else."

"Got to be good sometimes," Dave said. "Can't stay lousy all season." Like the others except Don and Tubby, Dave was in his early twenties. He was a blond, untidy boy with a soft, rather childish mouth and a big nose peeling from the sun. His partner, Jimmy Hailon, was small and almost daintily built, with slick, thick black hair and a small black mustache. Don noticed he had hardly spoken a word since he came aboard, but he was already on his third bottle of beer.

"One guy it stays good for is that Red Holiday," Hal said. "I'd like to be able to fish alongside him steady."

"You could do it if you had a big enough boat to pack ice," Dave Swanson said.

Hal glanced at him, a little contemptuously, Don thought. "Yeah," he said. "And if I was as good a seaman as Red is. They don't come like him every day."

Dick Evans reached for another bottle of beer and opened it. "Don't see what he wants to pack that partner of his around for. That guy's a pain in the neck the way he sits and stares without talking."

"Red and he was together in the war," Johnny Smith said. "Tom Moore got shot up bad and Red kind of carries him."

"I still can't see it," Dick said.

Don knew Evans hadn't been in the war and he wanted to say, "Maybe you could if you'd been there." But he knew that could only come from someone who had been there, so he said: "Tom Moore's a good guy. He's kind of hard to get to know, but I guess Red knows him and that's why he likes to have him around."

Evans looked up at Don. "You could be right," he said. "Still seems kind of daft to me for a guy like Red who could get any kind of partner he wants. But I guess it ain't none of our business."

Johnny Smith asked Don, "How deep were you guys fishing out there this afternoon?"

"Fourteen and twenty fathom," Don said.

Dick Evans whistled. "That's even more'n we figured," he said. "Let's look at your hands." Don showed his hands. They were sore and hot from pulling line, but they were in good shape, without cuts or cracks. Evans examined them closely. "Using rubber over them. They're okay so far, but you won't keep that up for long. You can't pull twenty fathom by hand day in, day out, and have your hands stand up to it."

"I figure they ought to harden up," Don said.

Hal Stevens laughed. "You could be right at that. I've seen it go that way. Willie Keen used to pull twenty-five-and thirty-pound lines by hand all season. But mostly a guy's hands seem to give out. Salt water cracks 'em; then he gets cuts, and first thing you know there's poison in 'em."

"Hal's right, Don," Johnny Smith said. "You'd better get spools if you want to fish that deep."

Don looked across at Tubby. "If the fishing keeps this good, we're liable to be able to do just that. What say, Tubby?"

Tubby grinned contentedly. "That'd make us a real outfit," he said.

12

The fishing didn't stay good. For the next two or three weeks the *Mallard* fished steadily with the *Milltail*, the *Jamaica*, and the *Varga Girl*. Each night they tied together and ran back in to Hardnose Cove with what fish they had, and usually one of the boats had some beer aboard or a bottle of whisky. Don and Tubby had stopped drinking after the first night and no one had bothered them about it, to Don's relief. But the drinking increased steadily as the fishing got worse and it often went on long after the boats were tied up in the Cove. Several times there were the beginnings of quarrels, and once the *Varga Girl* kept away from the group for several days.

More and more frequently one or other of the boats would be very late starting out in the morning.

Don caught the feeling of hopelessness fairly quickly. He and Tubby had continued to fish deep lines and their hands were beginning to crack. As often as not they came in without enough fish to pay for their gas after being out from three in the morning until ten or eleven at night. Tubby remained even-tempered and cheerful, certain that things would pick up sooner or later, but Don became moody and short-tempered. He felt unsure of himself again, and he wanted to be able to blame someone or something to take the load off himself. One night he told Tubby: "We just haven't got what it takes to fish this place. We ought to pull out for somewhere else."

"Why don't we?" Tubby asked.

"Where would we go? It'd be the same story over again. If we could fish deep lines and pack enough ice to stay out there, I'd go try it out at the Big Bank, alongside Red Holiday."

Tubby had heard that before. Don liked to play with it whenever his conscience pushed him for not trying hard enough, but he always found excuses for not going through with it.

"We could pack enough ice for one day's catch, stay out a night and come in the next night,"

Tubby said. "That way we'd get the late evening and early morning fishing out there, when the fish are shallowest."

Don knew that, but he knew it would mean breaking away from Hal Stevens and the rest of them and he didn't want to do that. Talking with them, cursing the scarcity of fish, talking spoons and rigging and boats and engines always made him feel confident and cheerful again. "It wouldn't work out," he said. "We wouldn't get fish. Red fishes very deep."

"We could try it."

Something in the way Tubby spoke made Don look at him sharply. "Darn you anyway," he said. "You don't think I'm scared, do you?"

"No," Tubby said gently. "Just losing your ambition is all."

"Okay," Don's voice was angry. "If that's the way you feel about it, we'll go out there. Red's in tonight. I'll go down right now and talk to him."

"I'll come with you," Tubby said.

"Suit yourself," Don told him.

The lights were still on in the cabin of the *Falaise* and they found Red and Tom Moore and Happy down there playing crib. Red was glad to see them. "Come on in, strangers," he said, "and visit the old folks. We were just talking about you."

"About the guys that can't catch fish, I suppose," Don said bitterly.

Happy looked at him. "That's no way to talk to friends, Don."

"It's okay," Red said. "I know how he feels.

How are your hands holding up, Don? That's what we were talking about."

Don held his hands out. Red took them in his own, looked at the palms, then turned them over. He did the same with Tubby's hands. "You're a tough pair," he said. "But I think it's going to get you. There's darn few men can keep on pulling the weights you've been pulling and not have trouble."

"That's right" Happy said. "Why don't you fish shallow? You'd get your share if you was out there at daylight and kept at it till dark. Take a rest in the middle of the day, when the fish are deepest."

"Heck" Don said, "we're not making gas now."

"You'll never make gas with your spoons in the salt-water tub" Happy said. "You fold up and head in with that bunch of playboys every night just about the time you ought to be fishing."

Don deliberately turned away from Happy and spoke to Red. "We thought maybe we could pack ice for one day's catch and fish out at Big Bank overnight. Do you think that'd work out for us?"

Red hesitated. It was easy to see that he was weighing things up pretty carefully and Don wondered exactly what were the points he was balancing for and against. Then Tom Moore spoke, very quietly, as always. "We've been getting fish at ten fathoms and less mornings and nights, Red."

Red nodded. "I know. Pig lines and bow poles, pigs mostly." He spoke directly to Don and Tubby. "If you'd rig yourselves pig lines, you might do all right fishing shallow. I told you that before, Don."

Don flushed. He knew that what Red was saying made sense. Nearly all the boats fished pig lines—long lines with a balloon float that carried them well back from the disturbance of the boat's passage before they dropped down to leads and spoons. Even the boats with gurdey spools used detachable pigs on their steel lines and usually claimed that the pig lines caught two fish for one on the other lines. Neither he nor Tubby had known how to rig a pig line when they came up, and Don had not wanted to ask anyone how it was done. To cover the fact that he didn't know he had argued with Tubby that pig lines simply meant more hand-hauling and didn't fish better unless they were deep. There had seemed some sense in that when they were already fishing all the line they could by handhauling, but he knew that what Red was saying made his argument foolish. He felt trapped and angry, but he said: "We could rig pigs to fish ten fathom. It was just when we were trying to fish deep I couldn't see them."

"You should've been fishing shallow right along," Happy said. "Instead of trying to kill yourselves hand-hauling twenty-five pounds of lead."

Tom Moore smiled gently. "They made a darn good try at it, Happy. Give the boys credit."

Don had felt himself almost out of his difficult position without too much loss of dignity. Now he felt trapped again and small and silly. "We can do it," he said aggressively, "if anybody can."

"No, we can't," Tubby said. "At least I can't, and I don't think you're in much better shape."

Don turned on him. "Okay," he said. "Go ahead, quit if you want. You never want to tough anything out, anyway."

"Skip it, Don," Red said easily. "Tubby's not quitting anything except a sucker's racket. And you ought to have sense enough to do the same. Come on out with us and try it shallow for a few days. You won't break any records out there right now, but you'll make better'n your gas."

Don still felt raw and confused and he wouldn't look at Tubby. But he couldn't find a shred of a quarrel in Red's level voice. He managed to say awkwardly: "That's swell of you, Red. We'll be there." He stood up. "I guess we better hit the hay now."

Walking back along the float Don and Tubby didn't speak. As he stepped aboard the *Mallard* Tubby turned back. "Look, Don," he said. "I can get out if you want me to."

Don pushed past him, went down into the cabin, and switched on the light. Tubby followed. "Don't act more of a darn fool than you have to," Don said.

"You don't need to get sore," Tubby told him. "I know the boat isn't making enough for two of us, the way the fishing is now. And there ain't work for two men unless the fishing's pretty fair. I could make out some way."

"You could like heck. How?"

"Happy's looking for a partner."

Don was trying to kick a boot off. He stopped abruptly. "So that's how it is!" he said savagely. "You think Happy'll catch you more fish than I will. You'll go along with him just because he's getting a few. That's fine. You can't go too soon to suit me."

"That's not the way I mean it. It's just I..."

"Shut up! If you want to quit, go ahead and quit. Don't whine about it."

Tubby hadn't started to undress. He stood up and his usually red, cheerful face was pale and angry. "That's all I'm taking," he said. "You think you can act meaner'n a squid just because things ain't going good for you. I've had all I want and I'm pulling freight right now."

Don kicked his second boot away from him, slid his pants off, and rolled into his bunk. "That's swell," he said. "Can't be too soon to suit me."

13

Don woke to the ringing of his alarm the next morning, sat up, swung his feet over the edge of the bunk, and stopped the alarm. As he did so he had a feeling that something was wrong. Then he remembered his quarrel with Tubby. He switched on the light and saw Tubby's empty bunk.

For a few moments he felt terribly lonely, as lonely as he remembered feeling when he had first come up to live with Joe and Maud Morgan after the death of his father. Then he had a sudden sense of freedom. It was miserable to be getting up and moving about the boat with no one to talk to, vaguely uncomfortable to think ahead to the day without Tubby. But it was good to be free to make any decisions he chose without risking Tubby's silent disapproval. Don made several decisions in rapid succession. First he decided that he would not go out to Big Bank with Red and Tom; he told himself that this was because Big Bank was too far out for single-handed fishing in a boat like the *Mallard*, and he refused to acknowledge, even to himself, that he was afraid to face what Red would have to say about the quarrel. Next he decided that he would tie alongside Johnny Smith's *Jamaica* to run out to the grounds. And then that he would rig two pig lines and try fishing shallow.

By the time he was dressed and had the stove going, Don was feeling excited and, in a way that he faintly mistrusted, happy. He started the *Mallard*'s engine, turned on her running lights, and went on to the float. The *Jamaica*'s lights were on and he saw Dick Evans come on to the float as he loosed the *Mallard*'s bow line. He waved and Dick waved back. "Step on it," Dick said. "We'll wait for you."

They tied together and Don went below to make coffee. He found he didn't much care for the prospect of admitting that he and Tubby had separated, even to Dick Evans. Dick had never seemed to care particularly for Tubby, or for anyone else for that matter except possibly Johnny Smith, and he certainly wouldn't be critical; but it was still a raw, cheapening admission to have to make. It reminded Don of having to face his friends after having been caught out in some not particularly admirable crime at school. He made the coffee and started some bacon frying, then went up. They were out of the Cove heading down toward Sad Point, and daylight was slow in coming. Dick was steering from the *Jamaica*'s pilothouse and Don went in and stood beside him.

"Looks like a change in the weather," Dick said. "We'd better keep somewhere close to the point till we see how she's shaping up."

A little breeze was coming up the channel toward them, just enough to slap wavelets against the boats. "Think it's going to blow hard?" Don asked.

"Your guess is as good as mine, but I'd say not today." He swung the wheel to meet a tide-rip. "We better eat soon. I'll go kick Johnny out. Tubby still pounding his ear?"

This was the time it had to be said. "Tubby quit me. Went with Happy Jackson."

"The heck you say," Dick spat over the side. "Oh, well, you're just as good off without him. Fishing's slow right now and Tubby's no ball of fire, for company or for fishing. Grab the wheel while I go roll that Johnny out."

Don found himself not liking this calm disposal of Tubby any too well, but before he could think of anything to say Dick had disappeared below. He peered ahead through the gray morning light, trying to pick out Sad Point.

They were round the point before they had finished breakfast. The breeze was still very light and Johnny said, "Where'll we hit for?"

"I figure to cut loose and start in any time now," Don said.

Johnny looked at him. "Scared?"

Don laughed. "No," he said. "I'm going to try it shallow and this is as good a place to start as any. I'll likely work as far up as you do later in the day."

"Okay," Johnny said. "Let's go. We'll pick you up on the way in."

Dick Evans freed the *Mallard*'s lines. Don slowed his engine and watched the *Jamaica* draw away. For a while after that he was busy, letting his poles down, checking spoons and gear, feeding his lines out. The light was still gray and dim when he had them all fishing, and he felt a thrill of expectancy in himself that he had not known since the first day or two of fishing at Pendennis Island. The whole day was ahead of him, he was fishing his gear in a new way, and he meant to try water he had not tried before. Above all, he was responsible only to himself; his decisions and choices would all be his own.

Don knew that some of the boats had been making small catches of cohoe salmon close in to shore along the west coast of the island. He had rigged smaller spoons, shortened his lines to about nine fathoms, and he meant to hunt fish as close to the beach as he dared go.

The new pig lines, carried well back from the boat's disturbance by their floats, caught for him almost at once. He pulled them and brought in two fish on each. The smart thing, he knew, would be to turn back and work over the good place again— but he had set his mind on working gradually up toward Sudden Point along the coast line, fishing close to the kelp wherever it grew or even inside it if there seemed to be water enough. So he held on his course. It began to rain and the wind freshened a little until the *Mallard* was lifting and swaying to the throw of small waves that were gradually building into an uneasy swell. Don went down into the cabin and pulled on black rubber pants and coat over his clothes. Back in the cockpit again he huddled over the tiller and watched his lines.

As the rain closed in he could see no other boats near him. He pulled another fish on the inside pig line as he trolled past a patch of kelp, but he had lost much of his early hope and excitement in the day ahead. He found himself thinking of what Tubby would be saying or doing if he were there, of the argument they would probably be having about the possibilities of the weather and the chances of fish.

The weather, Don thought, was setting toward trouble. The rain was cold, the clouds were drearily low, and the wind held steadily from somewhere a little west of south; there was something threatening in the feel of it and in the slap of the little waves against the *Mallard*'s hull. Tubby, Don felt pretty sure, would have been against trolling so close to shore with that wind almost abeam. And Tubby would have wanted to turn back over the place where the pig lines had first caught fish. Tubby didn't like taking long chances of any sort, Don told himself, and it was a good thing he was out of the way.

As he looked along the shore line ahead Don saw another boat through the rain and mist. It was trolling and at first he couldn't recognize it; then he saw it was old Jake Heron's *Blue Grass*. Jake was a gray-haired, gray-faced, middle-aged man who kept very much to himself. His boat was clumsily built and clumsily rigged, with an ugly square cabin, like a flimsy box, perched far forward. His trolling poles were short and thick and carried big heavy cattle bells instead of the little round bells that most of the trollers used. Old Jake was a farmer who had taken to fishing during the summer months. He was obstinate, clumsily inventive, hard-working, and used to hard times. He had never asked for advice or help and if anyone ventured to offer either he would grunt a surly rejection. In time most of the trollers

125

had learned to leave him alone. They called him Old Cowbells, laughed at his crankiness and his improvisations, his awkward, underpowered boat and his farmer's approach to seamanship; but at the same time they had developed a tolerant respect for his independence and determination and for the mixture of courage and ignorance that brought him north each year to match the ugly little *Blue Grass* against the storms and chances of open water.

Don had spoken to old Jake no more than half a dozen times in the weeks he had known him. He thought of him tolerantly and patronizingly as Old Cowbells and joked about him, none too kindly, with the other trollers. But now he found he was glad to see the *Blue Grass* ahead of him, glad because it was a lonely gray day in the rain and mist with the strengthening wind; a little irritated because it seemed wrong that Old Cowbells should have the nerve to be fishing his haywire little boat in a place where Don had just begun to feel that the *Mallard* might have no business on a freshening wind.

The *Mallard* was trolling a little faster than the *Blue Grass* and because he was lonely Don gave her another notch on the throttle. It would be pleasant to come alongside and shout something across to Jake even though the old man would probably give no more than a surly grunt in reply. They were working up inside a line of rocky islets that lay across Sully Bay, south from Sudden Point, and

Don swung the *Mallard* a little more over toward the islands to avoid crowding the *Blue Grass*. Very suddenly and loudly the bells on the port side pole jingled. Don yanked the throttle back, the *Mallard* heeled and swung over, a line broke, a pole cracked and shuddered. Don was in the pilothouse by this time. He had the engine going astern, but the *Mallard*'s way was too much. Her bowlines caught, then her starboard lines, before he had her stopped. The *Blue Grass* was disappearing into the mist again as Don went out on deck to check the damage.

He saw at once that the pole was badly cracked. Both the port lines and one of the starboard lines were broken. The bowlines seemed to be still fast in the bottom. He shrugged his shoulders hopelessly and kicked angrily at the side of the pilothouse. "Of all the hayseed tricks," he told himself. "Old Cowbells himself wouldn't pull one like that."

Even inside the partial shelter of the little islands the wind was still freshening and Don knew he had to do something. He took in the remaining starboard line, then went into the pilothouse and reversed the *Mallard* gently until he had strain on the bowlines. They did not come free. He ran ahead on them and they were still fast. For ten or fifteen minutes, in the rising swell and sea, he tried to save them. Then he knew it was hopeless and used the boat's power to break them. Except for the cracked pole, his loss was not really serious. His lines were rigged in gradually tapering strength from poles to bottom lead, so all except one had broken well down. One, unaccountably, had broken near the pole and its unweighted end trailed forlornly in the water.

The cracked pole was serious trouble. It could probably be spliced, but a spliced pole is clumsy and unsatisfactory. The chance of getting another one, Don knew, was slim. And he knew the crack was his own fault. Tubby had suggested weeks before that they should rig short pieces of breaking line on the tag lines that held the trolling lines out at their distance on the poles. Don had argued that the light line down deep would break if they hit trouble and that anyway they were not fishing near bottom. As he brought in his broken lines he could feel tears stinging in his eyes. He kicked the *Mallard*'s throttle full ahead and wrenched the wheel over. For a moment he felt like running her full speed into the beach, climbing ashore, and leaving her there to break up in the steadily increasing swell. "I'm sick of the whole business," he said aloud. "There hasn't been a single thing go right since we left the river."

He looked about him at the little islands and the dim shore line and the driving gray mist of the rain. "It's a lousy country and a lousy racket," he said. Then he remembered the hope and excitement he had felt when they first came up to Pendennis

Island, and he felt foolish. He went forward, raised his main poles and brought in his bow poles. Back in the pilothouse, with the *Mallard* running back into the swells and the doors and windows closed against the weather, he felt better. He was through fishing for the day. Back at the Cove it would be calm and quiet. He could splice the cracked pole and there would be someone there to listen and be sympathetic. And in the evening the boys would be back and they could talk and plan the next day's fishing down in the *Milltail*'s warm cabin.

14

The bad weather of Don's first morning without Tubby blew up into a powerful storm that drove most of the trolling fleet back into Hardnose Cove by early afternoon. The *Jamaica*, the *Milltail*, and the *Varga Girl* were among the first to come in and all three tied along the float near the *Mallard*.

Don went aboard the *Milltail* as soon as she tied up. He wanted to tell someone about his bad morning and he knew Hal Stevens would be sympathetic. Hal was down tinkering with his motor, but he looked up as Don peered down from the pilothouse. "You beat us in," he said. "Get scared out there alone?"

"No," Don told him. "Caught bottom and cracked a pole."

"Too bad. You'll have plenty of time to fix it, though. This blow looks good for two or three days anyway."

The boat rocked as Johnny Smith and Dick Evans came aboard. Don moved down to give them room and all four went forward into the *Milltail*'s cabin. "Going to be a three-day blow," Dick Evans said. "May as well get set for a big party. Johnny'll put it on. It's his birthday tomorrow."

"Like heck I will," Johnny said. "A guy don't have to buy his own party. He's done his share just having the birthday."

Hal laughed. "Hardest work you ever did, being born, wasn't it, Johnny?"

"Well, it's a cinch I don't have to pay you guys for it. You weren't even helping."

"Let's not talk ourselves out of a party," Dick Evans said. "Not in weather like this anyway. We'll buy the party, Johnny, just so you lend us the birthday. What say, Don?"

Don was feeling better. The warm, easy companionship there in the *Milltail*'s cabin was what he had been hoping for without really knowing it. "Sure," he said. "Sounds right to me. We'll all give Johnny a party."

"It's a date then," Hal said. "We'll tell the rest of the boys to rally around, so long as it's still storming."

"It will be," Dick Evans told him.

Johnny Smith's birthday party lasted through two full days while the storm clouds raced high over Hardnose Cove, and though there have been wilder and fancier parties, most of the trollers who were there still remember it. The start was quiet enough. On the morning after Don and Hal and Johnny and Dick Evans had decided on the party, the *Jamaica* pulled out early to pick up supplies from Whale River, the nearest settlement of any size. Phil Eastey, who had a reputation as a cook, had promised to brew up a great clam chowder, so Dave Swanson and Jimmy Hailon pulled out in the *Varga Girl* to dig clams on the low tide at White Beach. The *Milltail* was to be the center of the party be-cause she had the biggest cabin and the best galley, and Hal Stevens had a big tarpaulin that he could rig over the after deck. Hal and Don spent most of the morning cleaning up the boat and rigging the tarpaulin.

Soon after noon the *Varga Girl* came in with her load of clams. Another boat had found crabs, and her crew boasted they would fix them up in a way that would make Phil Eastey's clam chowder only a minor incident in the party. Then the *Jamaica* came in with the supplies from Whale River and the party really started.

The *Milltail* was tied just astern of the *Mallard* with the *Jamaica* astern of her again and the *Varga Girl* alongside. Nearly the whole fleet was tied up in the Cove because of the bad weather, and news of the party had spread quickly among the other boats. Most of the fishermen were glad of something to break the monotony of waiting for the weather to clear, so they sorted out small presents for Johnny, wrapped them carefully, and brought them along.

Don found he was enjoying himself. Phil's clam chowder was very good. Someone had cooked up a gigantic beef stew. Both this and the chowder lasted through the whole evening. The crabs disappeared quickly, but people kept turning up with offerings of cheese or bacon or biscuits or cake to keep the party going, and all four boats soon had food piled on every ledge and shelf and flat space that wasn't being used for sitting. The *Varga Girl* was making coffee, four pots on the galley stove, two more on the portable gasoline stove, constantly refilled. After a while Dave Swanson began lacing the coffee with rum, but it was evening then and that was the first drinking that had been done, though the *Jamaica* had brought plenty of everything back from Whale River.

The *Milltail* had been uncomfortably crowded with all the coming and going, but the visitors gradually drifted away to continue the party on other boats. The cabin was full of smoke and dirty plates and cups. Don was sitting on a bunk, feeling sleepy and full. He was missing Tubby a little, but at the same time he felt comfortable in the companionship of the men he was with. He was holding his mind away from the thought of going back to the *Mallard* alone.

Then Dick Evans said: "Well, boys, we can't let her die like this. It's still daylight and this is Johnny's birthday."

Johnny had made a speech at the height of things and hidden himself in a corner ever since. "Let it go, Dick. Let's all relax and be comfortable."

Dick shook his head. "No," he said. "No can do, Johnny. We've got to get the place cleaned up, have a couple of drinks, and get some music going. Why, there's a lot of the boys haven't been along yet—Happy, for one, and Tubby Miller. And Gerry Temple. And the *Falaise*'ll be in tonight for sure. Old Red'll want to be in on it."

"We ought to get some girls and start a dance going," Hal suggested. "Why didn't you bring some back from Whale River, Dick?"

"Johnny don't like girls," Dick said. "It's his party." Everybody laughed because Johnny's love affairs were a constant and complicated succession.

"He doesn't have to like them," Hal said. "They like him. They love his pretty brown curls."

Johnny swung a foot at him and they wrestled from the bunk to the floor in a clatter of dishes. Don stood up to get out of the way and Dick Evans grinned across at him. "May as well start on the clean-up, Don, while the kids play."

Don found himself liking Dick Evans more and more. Usually Dick was a little short and offhand, inclined to say hard, disconcerting things. His dark face and heavy eyebrows emphasized his manner, making him seem surly, almost dangerously ill tempered. Tonight he was cheerful and friendly and his dark strength made for confidence rather than fear. As they were straightening up the cabin and washing the dishes, Don asked him: "What do you think about splicing a pole, Dick? Can a guy make a job of it?"

"Sure, you can splint it up so it'll hold okay. It's kind of clumsy and awkward-looking, though. A new pole's a whole lot better."

"Even green?"

"So long as it's cedar. Green fir is too heavy and you won't get spruce around here. You can get all kinds of good cedar poles over on Queen Island, right in the entrance to Butcher Inlet."

"Might run over there tomorrow if the weather's still bad," Don said.

Dick laughed. "You can plan on it. Nobody'll be fishing tomorrow, the way the party's shaping up now." They were in the galley and Dick jerked his head toward the main cabin as he spoke. Gerry Temple and two other men Don didn't know had come in. Jimmy Hailon had brought out a bottle of rum and half a dozen of them were toasting Johnny's birthday. Don and Dick went in and Jimmy picked up the bottle.

"How'll you have it? Hot with butter?"

Dick nodded. "Sure. That's the only way."

"How about you, Don?"

Don smiled awkwardly and shook his head, but Johnny Smith said: "It won't hurt you, Don. You can't turn down a drink when a man asks you on his birthday."

"I don't like the stuff," Don said. "Otherwise I would. No offense, Johnny."

Johnny stood up and put an arm round Don's shoulders. "Don's a good scout," he said to the others. "We wouldn't lead him astray, would we, boys?"

Everybody laughed good-naturedly and Jimmy Hailon said, "I'll bet you never tried hot buttered rum, did you, Don?"

"No," Don admitted cautiously. "But I don't like the taste of hard liquor."

"You'll like a good rum drink," Dick said. "It doesn't taste like whisky at all. Johnny'll let you dump it after you've drunk his health, won't you, Johnny?"

"Sure," Johnny said. "I'm never going to get sore at old Don."

So Don found himself drinking Johnny's health in hot rum. It had a heavy, sweet taste that was pleasant enough and he liked the way it burned in his chest as he swallowed it. He drank Johnny's health and sat comfortably in a corner, nursing the warm mug.

Gerry Temple began to play his mouth organ and Dick Evans sang. Dick's voice was good, rich and deep and strong, and he had learned old Welsh songs that could stir the blood. Don sat and listened and let the songs reach into him.

After a while Dick stopped and Jimmy mixed more rum. Don's mug was still half full and they let him hold on to it as it was.

"Sing something else, Dick," Johnny said.

"Later," Dick told him. "Don't wear a good man down. It's early yet."

"You're right it is," Hal Stevens said. "We promised ourselves a two-day party and we've hardly got a start on it."

"What's for tomorrow?" Gerry Temple asked. "More clams? I remember once down at Bitter Harbor we got a steer and barbecued it on the beach for a party. That'd be okay."

Hal laughed. "You'd go a long piece to find a steer around here. The boys tried to get steaks up at the settlement today, but they didn't get to first base."

Dave Swanson said one word, "Venison."

Dick Evans took him up on it. "Out of season, no deer around, you wouldn't want to eat one as soon as it was killed anyway. Better go hungry on rum if that's the best you can think up, Dave."

"Mowitch steak eats good if you pound it a bit," Dave said. "And there's plenty of it on the hoof up Butcher Inlet."

Don had been listening closely. Somehow talk of deer hunting seemed good to him in the midst of all this water and boats and fish. There was the smell of the woods in it, of wet earth soft underfoot, the brush of leaves and branches against clothing, the friendly feel of rifle stock against the hand, the sharp imprint of a fresh track on a side hill trail.

Then Jimmy Hailon said: "Dave's right. Fresh venison is okay if you handle it right. I bet Don here could pick us a good buck. How about it, Don?"

The question matched Don's own thoughts so closely that it startled him. "Heck," he said, "I don't know the country. Anyway, it's out of season."

"You don't have to worry about that up in this neck of the woods," Dave said. "You could keep mowitch aboard steady and nobody'd catch up with you."

"That's not the way I heard it," Don said. "They keep pretty good track of that sort of stuff."

"What's the matter?" Hailon asked. "Scared? The way Tubby tells it you're woodsman enough to fool all the game wardens in BC."

There was something more than kidding in Hailon's voice, something close to a sneer that Don didn't like. Dave Swanson said: "Don's not scared, Jimmy. He don't know the country and he don't like to break the law."

Both Hailon and Swanson laughed at that and some of the others joined them. Don felt himself the center of attention and it made the blood pound in his throat uncomfortably. He had known that neither Hailon nor Swanson liked him particularly, but there had never been anything close to an open break between them. He said awkwardly, "Nobody wants an out-of-season buck."

"No?" Jimmy said. "We do. It ought to be simple enough for a great hunter like you to pick one up. Or maybe they're just easy meat down where you come from. That's how lots of reputations get started."

Gerry Temple hadn't sensed the tension in the discussion. "How about it, Don? Why don't you get out there tomorrow and show Jimmy up?"

"Not Don," Jimmy said. "He's not doing anything the law wouldn't like. Not even taking a drink."

Dick Evans hadn't laughed. He sat forward now, his huge shoulders hunched over his squat body. "Cut it out, Jimmy," he said. "Relax. We're all friends here. It's Don's own business what he wants to do or doesn't want to do."

"Now he's got you doing it," Jimmy said. "It's getting to be a regular Sunday School around here."

But they went on to talk of other things, and though Jimmy's bottle and two others were empty when the party broke up, there had been no real quarrel.

Don was half asleep as he took off his clothes and rolled into his bunk, but his mind was on deer hunting again and he was remembering what Jimmy Hailon had said. As he switched out his light he could feel the woods about him and when he closed his eyes he was searching for the movement of a gray shape among the green and brown of tall timber. "A man could take a walk in the timber and see what he ran across," he thought. "Maybe it wouldn't be too easy to get a buck up there, at that."

15

Don had not set his alarm clock, but habit woke him early the next morning. He could tell from the *Mallard*'s slight movement that it was still blowing hard outside and for a few minutes he lay on his back in the bunk, thinking over what had happened the previous evening. He intended to follow Dick Evans' advice and go up to Queen Island to look for a cedar pole. Beyond that he allowed himself to make no final decision, but he thought of the woods as they would be on such a day as this— dripping wet, soft underfoot, with the heavy wind high in the treetops and the thought stirred him out of bed.

With the wind astern he made the run to Queen Island in a little over two hours. He took the *Mallard* around and into the narrow passage between the island and the north shore of the inlet and found without difficulty the sheltered bay that Dick Evans had told him about. On the west side of the bay a small creek tumbled over a little bluff into the salt water. Someone had set a short length of pipe into the rock so that part of the stream ran through it, and Don judged from the names of boats painted on the rock face that purse seiners and gill netters ran up there to take on water. He eased the *Mallard* in gently and found a place where he could step ashore with a line and leave her securely tied in deep water right against the rock.

Finding the pole was even simpler than he had expected from Dick's account. Small cedar trees seemed to be growing everywhere on the island and he found a thicket of tall, straight poles within a hundred yards of the boat. He cut one that was about five inches on the butt and found that it had plenty of clear length for what he needed.

When he had secured it aboard the *Mallard*, Don found himself almost disappointed that getting the pole had been so easy. He had counted on spending at least two or three hours in the bush, hunting for a good one. He looked around the bay, hoping to find a larger creek flowing in somewhere, but he could see nothing that looked promising. He looked out of the entrance to the bay and across to the north shore of the inlet. A mountain climbed steeply up from the salt water, through three thousand feet or more of green timber to scrub and bare rock. From the water's edge a red gash cut back through the green for several hundred feet and Don knew that handloggers had worked there. Otherwise, so far as he could see, the mountain was untouched. Don glanced up at the sky, felt the rain on his face, and saw that the clouds were still sweeping up from the south. He thought of starting the *Mallard*'s engine and running back to the Cove, then pictured Johnny's party slowly getting started again aboard Hal Stevens' boat—Jimmy Hailon and Dave Swanson sprawled in the cabin, Gerry Temple coming in and shaking water from his wet black rubber coat, other trollers crowding in to talk and smoke and drink. He knew that was not what he wanted.

Half an hour later he was climbing the handlogger's skid road. The *Mallard* was tied in the bay on Queen Island, safe with a shore line and a stern anchor. He had crossed in the dinghy, dragging it up the beach beyond tide mark. As he climbed over the wet logs of the skid road he felt suddenly free of worry, sure of himself again, at home. His thirty-thirty rifle was slung in the crook of his left arm, but he was not hunting. He had told himself that he would not hunt, that he wanted only to walk in the woods, to climb the mountain to the bare rock and the low clouds, and forget, for one day at least, that there were such things as trolling boats and salmon and salt water anywhere in the world.

He passed the end of the skid road and came into standing timber. It was small stuff, spaced out and hung with branches, split by bluffs and little slides, but he found good game trails climbing through the short salal brush and the going was easy. He thought of Tubby and found that, for once, he was glad to be without him. Tubby would be puffing and blowing and complaining about the climb. Tubby in the woods and Tubby aboard a boat were almost two different people.

As he climbed, the timber became sparser, the bluffs steeper and more numerous. The trail he was following led almost easily among them, well marked by the passing of generations of deer and goats. Once he saw a doe standing in the trail ahead of him and stopped to watch her until she turned quietly away and disappeared into a patch of scrub timber. Once his eyes caught a flicker of movement at the base of a bluff and he saw an old buck lying there on his sheltered bed, motionless except for an occasional betraying twitch of his ears. The wind was right and Don passed without disturbing him. There was a new thrill of confidence in that, the stronger because his right hand had made no move to the stock of his rifle.

He passed through a wraith of cloud and came out on open bluffs. He was sweating a little and soaking wet from the rain, but his breathing was calm and his body was easy and strong and triumphant. The wind rushed past him as it had not farther down on the slope, drove the rain against him, tore at his clothes and his hair. He turned and faced into it, looking out over the lower clouds to the gray water of Hughes Channel, its waves and whitecaps flattened and made tiny by distance. He could see down the channel to the northern end of Priest Island, below Pendennis Island, and between the racing clouds to the southwest he could see clear across Pendennis Island to the open water of Queen Charlotte Strait.

Don climbed a little higher, found shelter from wind and rain in a crevice at the foot of a bluff, and sat down to rest. He let himself think of his hurts, of the quarrel with Tubby, of the failure of the season so far and the strong chance that he would lose the *Mallard* to old Shenrock. None of these things seemed to matter so much as they had. He looked down at the *Mallard*, a tiny thing in the bay on Queen Island, and felt that he could go back and take her out and catch fish. Shallow fishing with pig lines. Early morning and late evening. Let the *Varga Girl* and the *Jamaica* and the others go in or go out when they wanted. The *Mallard* would fish early and late.

Then he thought of Jimmy Hailon and Dave Swanson again, in the cabin of the *Milltail*, and the thought sent a hot flush of anger to his neck and face. "I should have pasted that Jimmy," he thought. "Pasted him good." But he knew there hadn't been a real chance. Dick Evans had stopped it from going that far. "Darn Dick anyway," Don told himself. "He didn't need to horn in." There was confusion and raw hurt in this thinking and it grew in him instead of lessening. Hailon and Swanson had been telling him he was a punk kid, too young and too green for the part he was trying to play with the *Mallard* up there on the grounds. They resented him, wanted to show him up. Miserably Don admitted to himself they were at least partly right. He hadn't made the fishing pay even as well as Old Cowbells had. He had talked big and acted big and done very little except quarrel with Tubby and disregard Red's advice. "And if there's any good way out of that without looking softer than ever," he told himself, "I'd sure like to know it."

He stood up at last, looked out once more from the high place, then threw the rifle over his left arm again and started down the hill. He traveled fast and almost silently over the wet ground and into the wind. He was back among the small timber, almost halfway down, when he saw the buck. It was a good buck, fat and smooth, with horns gleaming fresh from the velvet, and it stood for a moment below him in the trail, surprised as he was. Then it raised its forefeet and swung away. Don jumped the rifle to his shoulder and fired, saw the buck plunge forward and roll out of sight down the hill.

Don followed at once, sure that he had killed, and found it lodged on the slope against the butt of a small tree. He bled it there and dressed it, and the sound of his rifle shot seemed still loud about him on the hill. He was shocked by what he was doing and had done, but he would not allow himself to think of it clearly. He thought for a moment of leaving the buck there on the hill, but that went against everything he had learned. It might be wrong to kill a deer out of season, but it was more deeply wrong to kill and waste meat. Don swung the buck's hind legs around the tree, then grasped one of the horns and dragged him down the steep part of the slope. When the slope grew easier, he shouldered the buck and packed it. Now that he had time to think, he knew he was scared. But he felt defiant too. Jimmy and Dave and the rest of them wanted a buck. They could have one and like it and keep their traps shut from now on. It was still daylight when the *Mallard* came back to Hardnose Cove, and the buck was in her hold.

16

oward noon of the morning after Don had killed the buck at Butcher Inlet, Happy Jackson's *Summer Duck* was drifting in the easy swell near Hideaway Rocks. It was a fine clear day after the storm, with only the lightest of westerly breezes and the dawn fishing had been good. Happy and Tubby had fished on through the morning tide, but had caught little after the sun was well up. Finally Happy had taken in his lines and cut the motor. "May as well drift a while and cook us up a decent meal," he said.

As they sat down to eat Tubby asked, "Did you see the *Mallard* pull out today, Happy?"

"No," Happy said. "She was still tied up when we got away. No light aboard either. I guess Don slept in. They likely kept up that party pretty late again last night."

"You think he'll get in trouble over that mowitch?"

Happy shrugged his shoulders. "I wouldn't want to bet one way or the other. They don't keep much track up here, but often there's a bull or a game warden around when you don't expect one. And the whole darn trolling fleet knows about that buck."

"You mean somebody might stool-pigeon?

"It happens." Happy reached for the pot and poured himself another cup of coffee. "But I wouldn't lose any sleep worrying about it. Why don't you forget about Don for a while and enjoy yourself, Tub? He'll be okay when he's had a while of running things for himself."

"It's easy to say that from where you sit," Tubby told him. "But I can't get away from feeling I quit him when things were going bad. Wouldn't be so bad if the *Summer Duck* wasn't getting fish. But we've made pretty fair the days I've been with you."

"Forget it," Happy said. "You didn't quit, you got fired. Don's a good kid and he'll come out of it in the end. You'll be back fishing with him before you know it. Only trouble with Don is he's not meant for this fishing game."

Tubby sat forward in astonishment. "How do you mean that, Happy? Don's good around a boat and he's learning pretty fast about fish. He gets some obstinate ideas, but he knows better most of the time."

"Only trouble is he don't really like fishing or boats," Happy said. "Don's a real smart boy and he can do most anything he sets his mind to, but he ain't made to be a fisherman any more'n you're made to be a preacher. Don's a woodsman and he won't never be really happy on the salt chuck."

"Gee," Tubby said, "that sure is a different way of looking at it. It's hard to think of Don not being tops at anything he tries out."

"That's just because you've always seen him where he was good." Happy stood up and began to pile the dishes into the sink "Take a look outside and see how she's drifting. We got time for a good sleep before we start fishing again, if we want. I know I do."

Tubby went up on deck, looked around, and came back down again. "We ain't moving much," he said. "And there's no other boats anywhere near us. What'll we get tonight? More springs?"

"Likely. Pretty soon now we'll start getting cohoes in a big way, but I don't figure they'll be in on these tides we got now."

"Any chance there'll be another run of big springs?"

Happy nodded. "Should be more pretty soon. Down off Milbanke Sound we used to think we could recognize different runs, Nimpkish fish and Phillips fish and Rivers fish and so on. I don't know how much there was to that, but we used to get different runs passing through."

Happy kicked off his boots and stretched out on his bunk. Tubby thought hard for a minute or more, then he asked, "Happy, if you wanted to make her big, would you stick around here this season?"

"With my boat and rigging, sure," Happy said. "We're picking up springs and a few cohoes right along, not making big money but getting by. There's some cohoes coming in, that's for sure. If it's a big run, we can still make a clean-up. Even if the run's small and late, we'll be getting by and a little better. Start chasing around this late in the season and you're liable to miss out every place."

"How about the West Coast?"

"West Coast is for boats like Red's and bigger. You want to pack ice for ten days or two weeks. To be rigged like the rest of them these days it takes automatic pilot and first-rate gurdey spools, good navigation—even radar for finding depth. You'll come to all that sometime, but it's not for an old guy like me. Takes young blood to learn gear like that." Happy wriggled his toes in their gray wool socks, put his hands behind his head, and lay watching a disk of reflected sunlight that danced on the ceiling of the cabin with the boat's easy movement. "Don Morgan could learn all that stuff, but he won't. Don hasn't found himself yet, but when he does it won't be fishing."

Tubby was listening to the sound of an approaching diesel. The boat was running at something near her top speed and he was pretty sure it was the *Falaise*. "Hear that?" he asked Happy.

"Sure. It's Red and he ain't wasting any time."

"I better go up," Tubby said.

He went on deck and watched the *Falaise* come close and slow down. Happy came up beside him. Tom Moore brought the *Falaise* almost alongside. Red was out on deck.

"Say, Tub," he said, "know anything about Don killing a deer yesterday?"

"That's what he did," Tubby said. "Up Butcher Inlet."

"I guess it's right what we heard then. The cops picked him up this morning and took him and the *Mallard* up to Whale River."

"The heck you say!" Tubby felt suddenly cold in the bright sun. "How bad is that?"

"Plenty," Red told him. "They're liable to confiscate the boat. We're going up there to see if we can help out. Want to come along?"

"Better go, son," Happy said. "You may not be able to do much, but he'll sure be glad to see you."

Don sat waiting inside the police office at Whale River. The judge and the game warden had gone into the courtroom and he could hear their voices through the closed door. A tall provincial policeman wearing high brown boots, greenstriped khaki breeches, and a khaki shirt with a green tie was sitting at a desk piled with papers. It was two hours since the game warden had brought Don up from the wharf where the *Mallard* was tied alongside the game boat, but the tall policeman had not yet spoken a single word to him. Now he looked up from the desk and said: "Doesn't feel so good to get caught at it, does it?"

"No," Don said miserably. "What'll they do?"

The policeman shrugged his shoulders. "The judge is liable to be pretty sore. You fishermen break game laws all the time just because you figure you can get away with it."

"I never killed out of season before."

"That's what they all say," the policeman told him. "You look like a good enough kid though. Stand up like a man and tell a straight story when you get in there. That's the best chance you've got."

The courtroom door opened and the game warden came out. He was a big, broad, red-faced man who moved quickly and softly. "Go on in, son," he told Don. "Stand in front of the desk and don't forget to speak up. He's a little deaf."

Don went through the door, hesitated, then walked across and stood in front of the desk. He found himself looking down at a bald head bowed over a blue paper. The judge was a little round man, wearing a black coat, a very clean white shirt, and a black bow tie. Don stood there in silence for what seemed a very long time. The game warden came in, stood beside the desk, and cleared his throat. Without looking up the judge reached forward, grasped an open book that was lying on the desk, and drew it back on top of the blue paper. The game warden cleared his throat again. "Are you ready to begin, your honor?"

The bald head nodded twice. The game warden stood at attention, his chest out, and said in a clear voice: "Order in court. I now declare this juvenile court open in the name of His Majesty the King."

The judge pushed his chair back a little from the desk and looked up at Don. He had a big face, full, but deeply lined, with heavy pouches under the eyes. His nose was small and round, his mouth was wide but thin-lipped, with a deep line running from each corner to disappear in his square chin and reappear directly under it in two parallel folds of skin that ran down behind the black bow tie.

The eyes were small and brown and very sharp, at odds with the expressionless line of the mouth. Don liked the face and instinctively respected it, but he thought immediately, "He's like a frog, an old, wise, patient frog."

When the judge spoke he growled and cut his words short and clear; it was not too unlike the croaking of a frog, but it was a good voice and it carried a lot of authority. "Pay attention, young fellow, I'm going to read the charge over. Then I'll hear what the game warden has to say. Then you'll tell me your story. Nobody with you in court?"

"No, sir," Don said.

"Where're your parents?"

"I'm an orphan, sir."

"Guardian? Who's responsible for you?"

"My aunt and uncle," Don said. "Mr. and Mrs. Joe Morgan down at Starbuck River, near Bluff Harbor."

The judge turned sharply to the game warden. "You know them?"

"Yes, your honor. They're very fine people. Old settlers. Everybody knows Joe Morgan and respects him."

"I don't," said the judge shortly. "What's the boy doing up here without any friends?"

"He's got friends, your honor. They were out on the fishing grounds."

"Why didn't you wait and bring some of them up?" He turned back to Don without waiting for an answer. "You want to go ahead and hear this without waiting for your friends?"

"Yes, sir," Don said without hesitation.

"I'll hear it," the old man said. "But if I don't like the way it looks I may withhold judgment or sentence until I get hold of somebody. Understand?" And again without waiting for an answer he went on to read the charge from the blue paper in front of him. Then he told Don to sit down, swore in the game warden, propped his elbows along the arms of his chair, folded his smooth hands across his belly and settled himself to listen.

The game warden gave his evidence in precise, official language: acting on information received—proceeded by water to Hardnose Cove arriving there 4:30 A.M.—identified boat of accused—went aboard to conduct search—accused sleeping, aroused him, warned him—found deer in after hatch—recently killed—placed accused under arrest, warned him again, accused said...

Don watched the judge's face. He remained without a flicker of expression, except that the head was cocked a little on one side to listen. The old man made absolutely no move throughout the evidence, but once he growled sharply, "What was that?" and made the game warden repeat a sentence. When the game warden had finished his story, the judge opened his mouth and closed it, then turned his bright eyes on Don. "All right, young fellow, you've heard him. Now what have you got to say? Speak up."

Don stood up, shuffled his feet, looked down, and could find nothing to say. Everything he had thought of while waiting was muddled in his head and time was pounding at him. He heard the old man say, "Keep still and hold your head up."

He looked up. The judge said: "You're not a criminal, boy. Don't act like one. What happened?"

So Don told his story. He left out the part about Jimmy Hailon and Dave Swanson and started in with the trip to Queen Island to search for the pole. He told the old man about his walk up the mountain, about the buck lying under the bluff, and said that he hadn't meant to hunt.

"Why pack the rifle then?"

Don hesitated. "For company, I guess, your honor. Sort of habit."

The old man turned to the game warden. "You said you've got the buck outside? I want to see it."

"In here, your honor?"

"Yes, yes. Bring it in."

The game warden brought the deer in and the old man got up and looked it over closely. Don saw him nod approvingly. "Clean shot in the neck. Good clean butchering job. Who taught you that?"

"My uncle, sir."

"Didn't he teach you not to kill deer out of season?"

"Yes, sir."

The judge went back to his chair and sat down again. For a moment he sat staring in front of him with his hands folded on his belly. Then he looked hard at Don and began to talk.

"You're lucky enough," he said, "to live in a country where there's game for everybody to hunt. You're lucky enough to have been taught the right way to hunt and kill game. It isn't your game. It belongs to everybody and you've just got a share in it, certain privileges. There are no privileges without obligations, and you've been taught the obligations. There isn't the slightest excuse for what you did. You're old enough to know better, you've been taught to know better, and you do know better." The dry, growling voice went on, biting deeper and deeper into Don's pride in himself and any defiance he might have felt. It was saying the things Joe Morgan might have said, but saying them with such utter contempt that Don wished he could turn and run away. Instead of that he had to stand there, looking into the old man's angry eyes, and take it. "You've got a share in something you're not man enough to share. You've been given a trust you're not fit to hold. If there are enough people like you there won't be anything to share, there won't be any trust to hold long before you're an old man." The judge's old, lined face didn't change in expression as he talked and his lips hardly moved, but he spoke the words clearly and in such a way that each one hurt as it was meant to hurt. He stopped at last, clamped his lips tight shut, and glared at Don. Then, abruptly he swung in his chair and looked at the game warden. "Well, game warden, he's guilty of your charge. What do you want me to do with him?"

17

As Don waited to hear his sentence he felt that he hardly cared about anything they could do. The things the old man had said had made him angry and ashamed; his mind had worked furiously to twist them away from what he had done, to make them unfair or untrue or simply foolish, but he found no help anywhere. The truth of the words stuck and hurt, cut his man-size posturings down to child-size thoughtlessness.

He hardly heard the discussion between the old man and the game warden about his sentence. Vaguely he knew that the game warden was asking for confiscation of his rifle and the judge was refusing that. Don wondered again about the boat, but there had been no mention of it and he began to be hopeful that it might not come up at all. He had no idea of what sentence he was open to, but it seemed hard to believe that the boat could be confiscated, even though Gerry Temple had said that it would be.

Finally the old judge turned back to him. "I suppose you're making money at your fishing," he said. "I'm going to leave you your rifle because it's clear to me that you are normally fit to have it and I think you will have learned from this experience. But I see no reason why you should not pay a fine. I'll set the minimum—twenty-five dollars and costs."

The game warden was holding another blue paper. "There's a second charge, your honor."

The judge waved his hand impatiently. "I know, I know. I don't want to hear it. Let the boy pay his fine and go."

"But, your honor..."

"Tear it up. Tell your department I wouldn't sign the information. Adjourn the court." The old man stood up and strutted out of the room.

The game warden looked at Don and smiled. "The old man's quite a character," he said quietly. "He's sized you up as a good kid and I'm inclined to agree. Don't ever come up in front of him again, though."

Don grinned. "I won't," he said. "He sure can bawl a guy out."

"What he told you is good sense and you got it cheap at the price. Don't forget it, that's all. Pay your fine out in the office and get on back to your fishing."

Don had a five-dollar bill and seventy-five cents left when he had paid the fine. He took his rifle, started down the road toward the wharf, and met Red and Tubby almost at once. Their faces were very serious and Red asked: "All over? We started out as soon as we heard. How was it?"

"Pretty rough," Don said. "But they let me off easy."

"How come they didn't take the rifle?" Tubby asked. "They generally do."

"I don't know. They talked about it, but he let me keep it."

"Nothing about the boat?" Red asked.

Don shook his head. He was still confused and didn't know whether to be thankful for his escape or resentful of some of the things the old judge had said to him. They stayed in his mind and had lost none of their power to hurt and reduce him.

"I don't think they can touch a man's boat," Red said. "Not just for that."

"Most of the boys think they can."

"I know. Darn sea-lawyers. A man shouldn't listen to them. What did they do? Fine you?"

"Twenty-five bucks," Don said. "And the old boy talked me into feeling lower than a snake."

"You had it coming," Red told him. "What did you want to do a crazy thing like that for? I suppose you let those beer parlor fishermen talk you into it."

Don flushed. "Nobody talked me into it. Can't a man think up his own ways of getting into trouble?"

"Doesn't seem much like one of the ways you'd dream up," Tubby said.

"Well, it was," Don said shortly. "And you can forget the lecture. I've had all I want of that stuff."

"Okay," Tubby said. "Okay." And they walked in silence down to the boats. Only as they went aboard could Don find it in himself to say: "Thanks a lot for coming up. A man gets to feeling plenty lonely in a setup like that." He spoke to Red, without quite excluding Tubby, and it didn't make him feel any better.

The two boats tied together to run back to the Cove and Tom Moore had a meal ready aboard the *Falaise*. After they had eaten Don went back to sit in the sun and steer from the *Falaise*'s trolling cockpit. In a little while Tom Moore came out and sat with him. They said little at first. Don noticed through his depressed concern with himself that Tom seemed stronger and more confident than he had a couple of months before. He was still spare and fine-drawn, but he was deeply tanned by the sun and salt water and the long muscles flickered healthily under the brown skin of his forearms as he moved. His hands were still nervous, but calmer than they had been, and his eyes were calmer, too.

"Did you stay out on Big Bank right through the storm?" Don asked at last.

Tom nodded. "The wind was bad, but she didn't kick up out there the way you'd expect, and we were catching fish off and on all through. We ran into the Hole that second night."

They were both silent again for a longish while. Then Tom Moore said: "Don't take it all too hard, Don. Anyone can run into a bunch of tough breaks. You've about had yours right now."

Don looked at him in astonishment. His first reaction had been to cut Tom off short as he had Tubby, but there was an understanding gentleness, a sharing of trouble, in Tom's voice that stopped him. He said, "It's mostly my own fault, I guess."

"That's the safest way to figure it, so long as you don't let it get you down. You want to remember that men aren't all the same, some'll do better at one thing, some at another."

"What do you mean by that?" Don asked.

"Could be that this fishing's not your racket. I don't mean you can't make a go of it if you make up your mind to. I know you can. But there might be other things that'd come easier."

"You mean I've balled it up so I should quit cold, right now?"

"No," Tom said. "Don't quit now. You've got to beat it. But when everything's under control, take a good look at yourself. See if you really like it the way you do some other things. There's no percentage in a man tying himself up to something he doesn't like, not at your age."

Don thought hard, staring off across the water for a minute or more before he answered. This was an angle he had never thought of before. It couldn't be right, he thought; I've always wanted a boat like the *Mallard*, always wanted to get away on my own and fish. It's a good life and I've always been good around a boat. Fishing's not so different from hunting; a guy has to do some of the same kind of figuring, only it's fish under water instead of animals in the woods. Then he thought of the way he had felt when he was climbing the hill on Butcher Inlet; and, way back beyond that, of how he had felt that night he and Tubby had gone up into the lagoon after pulling out from Viscount Channel.

"You mean I don't like fishing?" he said at last.

"Not necessarily," Tom said. "Just that you ought to check up on yourself and be sure that's what you want. There's plenty of other things a man can do."

"Such as what?" Don asked. "'Most anything else but fishing and trapping makes you a wage slave."

Tom laughed. "There are worse things. Did you ever think of going back to school?"

"After spending two years trying to talk my way out of it with Aunt Maud? I should say not."

"No," Tom said. "I mean it seriously. You're smart enough to go through college, and that can open things up if a man's got something on the ball."

"Not me," Don said. "I'm not the type."

Tom Moore stood up. "I wouldn't be too sure. Think it over. There's room for smart men in the world and a little education's no handicap."

"I'll think about it," Don said. "And the other. Thanks a lot."

Tom climbed up out of the cockpit. "I better see what Red's doing. We'll be in pretty soon and he said to let him know."

18

For a week after his trial Don fished alone. He followed his theory of working close to shore and fishing pig lines and he caught fish, but it was hard work. Once or twice he anchored overnight in the Hole, a rocky, shallow bay well up the west coast of Pendennis Island, rather than run back to the Cove. He had had time during the week to do a lot of thinking. Tom Moore's suggestion that fishing might not be his racket had been in his mind again and again. There were things about fishing, and even about boats, he admitted to himself, that he didn't like. That wasn't necessarily bad, he decided;

there are things about any job for a man to dislike. The real question was how the balance lay between things liked and things disliked

It was a far more important discovery that there were things about boats and fishing that didn't come naturally to him as they came to Tubby or Red or Phil Eastey or Happy. In the woods, around the farm, even in school, things that were hard and unnatural for Tubby came easily to Don. Here on the salt water Don often found himself up against things he only half understood—things like the plotting of a course on the chart, figuring tides, judging weather or the safety of an anchorage, things that Red or Tubby would have settled without more than a moment's thought. He told himself that experience had a lot to do with it, just as his own woods experience made him superior there. But he had an uneasy feeling that there was more in it than this, because he knew that when one of these problems faced him there was no drive of enthusiasm to help him solve it. He choked this feeling back, blocked it away from his clearest thinking, because he was not ready to accept what it meant.

He had almost given up worrying about saving the *Mallard* from old Shenrock, but he had not given up hope. That there was little enough to support his hope, he knew well. But the debt was still a challenge to him and he wasn't willing to yield an inch on it. There was a chance, he told himself, that the cohoes would come in well here at Pendennis Island, and a few weeks of good fishing could wipe out the debt. Beyond that it was no use worrying. By pulling out to hunt for fish elsewhere he would certainly lose fishing time, as well as the local experience he had gained, and there was no certainty that he would find what he was looking for. That had not been an easy decision to make. He would have been glad to get away from Pendennis Island, if only to be free of the shadow of his quarrel with Tubby, the memory of the deer hunt, and the certainty of running into Dave Swanson and Jimmy Hailon whenever he tied up at the Cove. But he knew it was a sound decision and he found satisfaction in it.

Altogether, Don felt, it had been a good week. But it had been a lonely week too, and he was glad to find space to tie behind the *Milltail* when he came in late on Saturday evening. Most of the boats were in. He saw the *Falaise* and the Summer Duck, the *Jamaica* and the *Kingfisher*. It had been a quiet fishing week, neither particularly good nor particularly bad, and the weather had been fair all through. Most of them would stay tied up over Sunday, Don thought, to check their gear and wash out a few clothes and catch up on sleep.

He cleaned up, changed his clothes, and went aboard the *Milltail*. Dick Evans and Johnny Smith were down there with Hal Stevens, playing three-handed crib. "Come on in, stranger," Hal said. "How's the fishing?"

"I've been getting by," Don said. "When's that cohoe run due in?"

Hal looked at his watch. "On Track 2, any time now. She's way overdue. Like that twenty-nine hand Dick's looking for to save a skunk."

"With the luck you've been getting it'll take more'n that," Dick said. "Hoyle used to say crib was a game of skill till he heard about you."

They heard footsteps up on deck and Red and Tom Moore came in. Red held a package out to Johnny Smith. "Figured you'd be here when there was nobody aboard the *Jamaica*," he said. "This is from Tom and me to make up for missing the birthday."

"You came at the right time," Dick said. "Johnny's fixin' for another party tonight, aren't you, Johnny?"

"No," Johnny said, opening the package. "I'm off parties for life. That one got me a stomach-ache from too much crab and clam chowder. It made you a grouch all week from a sore head. And it darn near put Don in the hoosegow." He got the wrapping off the package and saw what was inside. "Holy smoke, Red, you didn't have to give me those. That's too darn much."

Don recognized the smaller of two pairs of German field glasses he had seen aboard the *Falaise*.

It was like Red to do that, he thought, and like Tom, too. It was a fine present.

"Tom and I figured it was time they were put to work," Red said. 'We use the other pair all the time."

"Well," Johnny said, "I'm not handing 'em back. But it calls for a drink, maybe two."

"No more parties, Johnny," Dick said.

"That's for you. We don't all pack around sore heads for a week after every drink we take."

The crib game broke up and everybody settled down to talk. Gerry Temple and Phil Eastey came in. Gerry asked Don, "Were you fishing close inshore today?"

"Sure," Don said. "Right up against the kelp."

"See anything of Old Cowbells in there?"

Don thought for a moment. "No," he said. "Haven't seen him since the first part of the week. Why?"

"He sold his fish just ahead of me," Gerry said. "And, boy, did he ever have a load of cohoes. Here's me with a five-thousand-dollar boat and him with one I'd take if you gave me five hundred along with it. Me with just enough fish to cover the ice in the hold and him with a boatload."

Red laughed. "You'll have to get out where the fish are, Gerry." Gerry liked to fish off Canvasback Island, south of Big Bank, where Red fished mostly, and they argued freely about the

171

respective merits of their chosen places. "You want to know where your hayseed friend has been fishing?"

"Off Big Bank, I suppose," Gerry said. "It'd only take him one day to run out there and another to get back."

"That's right where he was. We saw him there Thursday morning, didn't we, Tom?" Tom Moore nodded. "And he stayed out till this afternoon. How did his fish grade?"

"They knocked down some of 'em," Gerry said. "But at least he had fish. The crazy old coot, going out there in that egg crate. They say the Lord looks after his own. I guess the old boy must be mighty close to rating a halo."

"He will be if he goes out there often," Dick said. "And a harp, too."

"No use telling him to stay away," Red said. "Especially when he's catching fish. He's a suspicious old crank and he'd figure we just wanted to scare off competition."

"Somebody ought to tell him, just the same," Phil Eastey said.

Hal Stevens got up to fetch more cups as Dave Swanson and Jimmy Hailon came in. "No use," he said. "The old boy's cussed as all get out. He'd just tell you to go peddle your papers."

"Who's that?" Jimmy asked.

"Old Cowbells—Jake Heron in the *Blue*

Grass," Hal told him. "The boys don't think he ought to be out fishing off Big Bank."

"Why not?" Dave Swanson wanted to know. "Let the old clown drown himself if he wants. He's fishing all hours of the day and night anyway—more like a Jap than a white man. If he had the boat and gear, he'd get the price of fish cut all by himself."

"I hear by the radio they're going to let the Japs come back to the coast," Dick Evans said. "Think that's right?"

"No," Hal told him. "They'll never let them back. Too much feeling against it."

"They better not," Jimmy Hailon said. "There'll be bloodshed if they do and I'll be one of the first to start it."

Don was only half listening. It was an old, old discussion, full of prejudices and half-truths and out-and-out lies that he had listened to a hundred times. A group of fishermen would get together, pile hearsay on hearsay, mix in a little fictitious personal experience and talk the thing up to a pitch of mob violence. He knew what Joe Morgan thought about it and he had liked the few Japanese he had known before they were moved from the coast during the war, but he had never fished against Japanese so he usually kept quiet. He was thinking now of how thoroughly he disliked Dave Swanson. For some reason that he couldn't figure out he felt that Dave was mainly responsible for his trouble over the out-of-season buck. There was something about Dave that one associated with trouble. Something wrong about the guy, Don told himself for want of a word that would express better what he felt, something of a sideways look about him, with the lank blond lock of hair that was always falling forward to the bridge of his nose. And Dave was the only one of them all who hadn't been halfway human after he got back from Whale River. Don enjoyed hating Dave across the cabin, and he hoped that sooner or later something would give him a chance to level the score against both Dave and Jimmy Hailon.

They were still talking about the Japanese. Building it up, Don thought, just the way Uncle Joe says they do, just the way the Germans built it up against the Jews. He watched Red. Red was standing in the doorway of the cabin, leaning against the frame, his head bent forward a little but still touching the ceiling. He looked very big and very relaxed as he listened and watched the faces of the speakers, and there was a tolerant smile on his lips that made Don think of a grownup watching children at play.

Dick Evans said: "I remember we had a tough time with them in the trollers' strike back before the war, but we got 'em stopped fishing in the end. Just the same, I don't think I'd want to see 'em back out here."

"A lot of it's politics," Hal Stevens said. "A cheap way for a politician to get him a few votes. They've even got cabinet ministers acting like clowns over it, for less than twenty thousand Japanese in the whole of Canada.

"I wouldn't want to fish alongside them again," Gerry Temple said. "They were mighty tough competition—goods boats and gear, living on rice and fish, out on the grounds day and night, ready to cut prices any time. They about wrecked the cod fishing that way."

Don noticed Happy Jackson standing beside Red in the doorway, listening closely. Happy said: "I fished cod alongside 'em and always made out good. They always treated me square and they were good fishermen. It was prices wrecked the cod fishing in the thirties, and she'd have gone the same way, Japs or no Japs."

Phil Eastey laughed. "That's okay for you, Happy. You always were a top cod fisherman. I never fished 'em myself, but I used to hear the boys talking about you coming back high boat from banks nobody else could find."

"One or two of the Jap boats found them with me," Happy said quietly. "And they were good to fish alongside of."

"There were some good ones," Phil said. "But a lot of 'em were pretty cocky. I figure the whole bunch of 'em would have turned against us if the coast had ever been invaded."

Dave Swanson had tried to break in several

times. Now he said: "You're darn right they would. That's what they were here for. Back in '41 one of them told me they'd have control of the whole of BC inside six months."

"Where was that, Dave?" Happy asked him.

"Out at Ucluelet."

"Didn't know you were ever there."

"Well, he told another guy and the guy told me. You can't trust any of them. They're all Jap citizens before they're anything else."

"They ought to load 'em all aboard a boat and ship 'em back to Japan," Jimmy Hailon said. "And it wouldn't hurt if she leaked enough to sink on the way." He turned to Red. "That wasn't what you guys went over there to fight for, Red, so a lousy government could let the Japs back in."

Red shrugged his shoulders. "I wouldn't know," he said. "There's some say it was."

"That ain't what Paul Marshall says. Paul was taken prisoner at Hong Kong and he says they ain't human beings at all. Like wild beasts, he said they were."

"Paul Marshall never told you that nor anything like it." Tom Moore was talking, quietly and evenly, from his seat in the forward corner of the cabin. Everyone looked at him. Don realized that it was the first time he, or probably anyone else there except Red, had ever heard Tom Moore speak out in a group. Jimmy Hailon jumped to his feet, but Tom said: "Sit down, Jimmy. I've talked plenty with Paul, and one thing he's sure about is that they had both kinds, good and bad, same as we did and the Germans did. He's told me some of the guards stuck their necks 'way out to give the boys a break, and some of them were tougher than they had any need to be."

"Did you ask him what there was most of?"

"Shut up, Dave" Hal told him. "Most of us'd just as soon hear what Tom has to say. He don't shoot his face off so much as some of the rest of us."

Tom went on without hesitation. "I'm good and sick of hearing folks back here tell returned men what they were fighting for. One big reason we went over there was because a little popeyed rat was encouraging German working people to talk and think just the way we've been talking here tonight."

"That wasn't quite the same, Tom," Dick Evans said mildly enough. "The Japs were getting dug in awful tight here on the coast."

"Sure it was the same." Tom was still talking calmly and easily, but Don noticed his hands were unsteady as he rested them on the table top. "And it's the same way as people in BC used to talk about Chinese or Hindus or Doukhobors before the war, and the way they will again. It's the way prairie people talk against Ukrainians and Ontario people against French Canadians. And it's got no place in North America. The biggest idea in this whole country, and the States too, is that people of any kind can come here and develop into good citizens. They can too. They have—Japanese and Chinese, Ukrainians and Czechs, Germans and French and English and Irish and Scottish. Some fit in quicker than others, but that's only because we give some a better break than others." He paused, but it was obvious he hadn't finished and everyone waited for him to go on. Dave Swanson moved and started to say something, but Hal Stevens glanced at him and he stopped.

"If you want laws passed that'll be rough on any small group of people in the country, you can get it done. Just holler loud enough, the way we coast people have about the Japs, and they'll pass the laws back in Ottawa. But any time you do that you've laid the way open for the same thing to happen to the group you belong to, and everybody belongs to some kind of a group. Remember Hitler used to check back to grandparents and great-grandparents to find his phony non-Aryan blood."

Don was watching Red Holiday. Red had put one foot up on the edge of a bunk and was leaning forward with his elbow on his knee, listening to every word. Generally when Red watched Tom his eyes had a worried, almost fatherly look; but now they were attentive and respectful.

"All this stuff people drag up against the Japanese," Tom was saying. "You can check quickly enough whether it's fair or not. People want to say they'd have been traitors if there had been an invasion. Do you think plenty of Germans wouldn't have gone over to Hitler if he had come here? People want to say the Japanese are cruel in ways white people couldn't be. I tell you the Japanese never thought up anything like the German murder camps, like Buchenwald and Belsen. They never got around to planning the scientific murder of millions of people. Yet nobody tries to say Germans can't make good Canadian citizens—we know they can. Think that over for a little while and you'll know there's nothing fair in the stuff we try to build up about the Japs. The reason we don't like them is because they were tough competition."

Tom's voice was strong and clear as Don had never heard it. Everyone in the crowded little cabin was listening to him and Don knew somehow that Tom was talking from above them; he was not a part of the untidy argument that had been going on before he spoke, but a clear voice from outside it, collapsing half-truths and destroying lies.

Dick Evans said: "I know that's right, Tom. But I still don't think they played ball with the white fishermen. They scabbed on us when we were striking and they'd take low prices any time, some of them. I don't think the fishermen'd be against them if it hadn't been for that."

"That's happened in other industries," Tom said. "And been taken care of. You weren't properly organized in those days. We are now. We bargain for

179

prices even before a season starts. Another thing, the white fishermen forced the Japs back into a tight group because they wouldn't accept them. The union'd have to watch that, too. But those things aren't the point. What matters is people hating a whole group of other people without stopping to think it's made up of people exactly like themselves, with the same kind of feelings and hopes and fears. Worse than that, making up lies to prove they aren't the same." He looked across at Jimmy Hailon and Dave Swanson. "That's where you came in, boys. Remember?"

Dave shrugged his shoulders and turned away. Jimmy said: "You might be right. I wouldn't know. But I'm still reaching for the old thirty-thirty when the first one shows up."

"It'll be quite a while," Tom said gently. "Guys like you have seen to that." He looked down at his watch. "Heck, Red, it's time to hit the hay. First time I've talked like that in years."

Don watched them go out together and for several moments no one said anything. Then Dick Evans stood up. "Well," he said, "if anyone had told me an hour ago I'd listen to a guy talk for the Japs and like it, I'd have called him a liar. And if he'd said the guy'd be Tom Moore, I'd have figured he was crazy as well as a liar."

19

Sunday was a hot, still day, but few boats went out. Don had wakened at the usual time, then rolled over and slept in until almost nine o'clock. It felt good to get up then, make a pot of coffee and some breakfast, and realize that he had a clear day ahead to clean up the *Mallard* and get her in shape for another stretch of fishing. The past week had made some money, even though not the sort of money that would payoff old Shenrock, and putting gear in shape made sense when there was every reason to suppose that the week ahead would be at least as good.

Halfway through the morning Red Holiday came along to the *Mallard*. Don was rigging the pole he had cut on Queen Island and Red helped him, then sat down to roll a cigarette and talk in the sun. The *Varga Girl* was tied alongside the *Mallard* and he nodded towards her. "They around?"

"No," Don said. "Haven't seen a sign of 'em."

Sleeping in, I guess. They were at it pretty strong when I pulled out last night."

Red rolled his cigarette very carefully, taking far longer over it than he usually did. Don watched in silence, knowing that Red had something important he wanted to talk about. Red lit his cigarette, then he said, "Look, Don, you remember the night Tom tried to go overboard in his sleep?"

"Sure do," Don said.

"It's because you saw that I want to talk about this other. You remember I told you Tom was acting out a dream about what happened at Falaise when he tried to go overboard? And that there was something bad in there he had to cut loose from?" Don nodded. "Well," Red went on, "I believe he did it last night."

"The heck you say!" Don could feel the excitement in Red's quiet words. "What happened?"

"You saw it. Tom's been getting better these last weeks, a whole lot better. But you never heard him talk the way he did last night, did you? You never heard him say more than a word or two nobody paid attention to when he was in a bunch of men like last night, did you?"

"No," Don said, "I didn't. I could hardly believe it was him when he first started last night. But after he got going it sure seemed natural enough, and it seemed natural enough for everybody to listen."

Red took a pull at his cigarette, then threw the butt overboard. "That was the same argument we got into the night before Falaise, a whole bunch of us from BC that were in the platoon together. It got kind of hot, too, and Tom was going along almost exactly the same line as he was on last night."

Don thought for fifteen or twenty seconds before he answered. He couldn't see at all clearly the connection between the argument and what had happened the day after it. "You mean you think the two are tied up, the Jap business and Tom's dream?"

"This morning Tom's just the way he used to be—sure of himself and right on top of things. That's the way he was last night aboard the *Milltail*. And that's the way he was the night before we went into action at Falaise. So far as I know he's never been that way in all the time between."

Don frowned in concentration. "I think I get what you mean," he said slowly. "There was something about the Jap argument, something bad, that stuck in his mind when he was fighting next day. Then it sort of stayed with him and he gets the dream more because of the argument than the fighting."

"Something like that," Red said. "There's some sort of a tie-up. And now that he's had it all out again, he's going to be okay. I'm keeping my fingers crossed anyway."

"Gee," Don said. "That's pretty swell, if it's right."

"It wouldn't surprise me if it isn't all squared away yet, though. Those things don't happen all in a flash and they don't straighten up all in a flash. But I thought you'd understand better'n anybody else after seeing Tom that night. I figure it'll be best if nobody seems to notice much about Tom's being different. And maybe it'd be just as good to stay off talking about Japs for a while unless he brings it up himself. You could maybe help out with that if you're around. And maybe keep the boys from saying anything about him being different. Likely most of 'em won't even notice, but one or two might, like Dick Evans and Hal Stevens."

"Dick and Hal'd do anything like that to help," Don said. "I'm sure glad you told me, Red."

Red fumbled for his pouch and began to roll another cigarette. "I got to wanting to talk about it awful bad," he said. "And I couldn't figure it'd be very smart to talk to Tom. How about yourself, Don? Why don't you and Tubby patch it up and get together again?"

Don hesitated. "Likely we will," he said. "Sometime. But there ain't much percentage in it right now, the way the fishing is."

"There's liable to be cohoes in any day now," Red told him. "It'd count to have two of you then. Better think it over." He looked at his watch. "Time I was back at the boat. Tom's got dinner cooking. Want to eat with us?"

"No thanks, Red. I got laundry to do. I'll get my own."

"Supper then?"

"Sure," Don said. "That'd be swell"

After Red left him Don put his clothes to soak, then went down into the *Mallard*'s cabin to start his own meal cooking. He stoked his little coal stove and put the pots on, then lay down on the bunk and picked up a magazine. As he lay there he heard Dave Swanson and Jimmy Hailon stirring aboard the *Varga Girl*. At first there was only the low murmur of their voices. Then one of them was working the wing pump on the sink. Don flipped his magazine away and sat up.

He was still sitting on the edge of the bunk when he felt the explosion. He could never remember afterwards that he heard it, except as a sound like rushing air. But he felt it as a dull, heavy blow on his back that threw him forward and banged the *Mallard* against the float. All fishermen know about gas boat explosions and Don knew instantly that the *Varga Girl* had exploded and would be on fire. He was through the *Mallard*'s engine room and out on deck in a moment. He heard the sound of feet running along the float behind him, but did not turn. His brain was working frantically, yet clearly, to take in what had happened.

The entire outer half of the *Varga Girl*'s cabin was blown out and flames were pouring through the gap, crackling at the pilothouse and the remainder of the cabin. For a fraction of a moment Don thought of the *Mallard*—to cut the lines, push the other boat away, and save her from the flames. But even while the thought was in his mind he was moving forward, stepping from the *Mallard* to the *Varga Girl*, searching for a sign of Jimmy Hailon or Dave Swanson. He went across the deck into the pilothouse and met a rush of flame that drove him back. Twice he tried again, gripping the scorching door jamb and trying to force his body against the heat, but flames leapt at his face, forced him to throw his hands up and close his eyes.

The thought was perfectly clear in his mind then that Jimmy and Dave were dead, but he knew also that he could not stop, that only seconds had passed since the thing had happened, that there could still be a chance and he must use it. He tore off his shirt and threw himself down on the deck, meaning to soak it in salt water and tie it across his face. Then he saw a head in the water. He drew his body into a crouch, plunged overboard, and came up swimming. Dave Swanson was swimming toward him. Dave was swimming strongly, Don saw, and he shouted to him, "Where's Jimmy?" Dave kept swimming and Don saw the expression of wild panic in his pale eyes. They were close to each other now and Don said: "Keep going. You can make it. Where's Jimmy?"

But Dave didn't answer. He swam past, blank terror still frozen in his eyes, and on toward the float. Don half turned in the water to follow him. He felt suddenly helpless and wrong. Dave was okay, but Jimmy must be back there in the burning boat, and Don had left him to die.

Don turned again, looking about him in the water. Then something flashed in the sun like a little smooth wave. Don drove himself toward it with half a dozen powerful strokes, found nothing, put his head under water and saw something below him. He dove, fighting down and down and down, until he reached out a hand and grabbed the back of Jimmy's shirt. The body lifted to his touch and he got a new grip, then started up. There was light above him, far up through what seemed an infinity of green water. The light was hurting his head, burning in his chest, but he knew he had to swim up to it. Suddenly the light was strong all about him and a moment later he was out in the air. He was still holding Jimmy and there was someone else with him. He tried to say, "Hello, Red," but he couldn't. Red said: "Well done, kid. You can let go. I've got him now."

Don looked at Jimmy and saw that Red was holding his head up. He loosed his own grip, shook his head, and dragged in another great breath of air. Then he knew Tom Moore was there as well. "Can you make it back?" Tom was asking. "I'll swim alongside of you. It isn't far."

Suddenly Don felt good again, so good that he laughed out loud. "Sure I can make it," he said. "Don't worry about me. Give Red a hand with Jimmy." But Tom swam alongside him back to the float and helped him up out of the water when they got there.

20

For a few minutes after he had been pulled up on the float Don lay flat on his back and took air into his lungs in breath after hungry breath. People were moving all about him and some spoke to him, but he kept his eyes closed and did not answer. He was content to be there, with the sun warm on him and people around to do whatever difficult things there were to be done. Then he knew his hands were hurting and suddenly his mind came awake again and he wanted to know a dozen things at once—whether Dave had got back to the float, whether Jimmy was alive or dead, where Red was, what had happened to the *Varga Girl*, what had happened to the *Mallard*.

He sat up abruptly and looked at his hands. Someone said: "That's the boy, Don. You'll be okay now.

"Sure," Don said, but he was looking out at the water. The *Varga Girl* was a couple of hundred feet from the float, still burning, with two other boats near her. The *Mallard* was still tied to the float, unharmed so far as he could see. A group of men were standing round something on the float twenty or thirty feet away. Don knew it was Jimmy and he stood up and walked over to the group. As he got there someone said: —"He's coming round. The water's out of him now." Don saw that Jimmy Hailon was face down on the boards of the float and Tom Moore was working over him; but Jimmy was moving.

Phil Eastey came up and stood beside Don. "There's one guy'll owe you every breath he draws from now on," he said. "Ought to make you feel pretty good."

"How did it happen?" Don asked.

Phil shrugged his shoulders. "Dave says Jimmy was lighting the gas stove. The boat must've been full of gas fumes from the bilge, though, leaky tank or something. You don't get two men blown out through the side of the cabin without something like that. You've got Tubby Miller to thank your boat didn't go too."

"Tubby?" Don said. "How's that?"

"He went aboard and cut the lines and pushed Swanson's boat out of there with a pike pole. Everybody else was too busy to think of it; between looking for you and Jimmy and trying to help Dave."

Don turned away and went over to the *Mallard*. He went aboard and down into the cabin, but there was no one there. He knew the *Summer Duck* was tied a little way ahead and he found Tubby there, lying on his bunk. Tubby said: "Hello, Don. I pulled out soon as I saw you were okay. Too darn much excitement around there. How's Jimmy?"

"Coming around," Don said. "I heard them say he's got some bad burns." He sat down awkwardly on the bunk across from Tubby. "Did you see Dave when he got to the float?"

Tubby nodded. "Tom Moore helped him in, then went back for you. Dave wasn't hurt any— just scared plumb crazy. Made me feel sick to my stomach just to look at him. That's why I came back here."

Don noticed again that his hands were hurting. He looked at them and saw for the first time that the backs were badly blistered. "For the love of Pete," he said, holding them up for Tubby to see. "Would you look at that?"

Tubby was off his bunk in a moment, reaching into a cupboard. "You crazy nut, Don," he said.

"Why didn't you tell someone? You didn't even get yourself dry clothes yet, either." He found what he was looking for in the cupboard. "Here," he said. "This tannic acid junk is good stuff. Smear it all over them. How in heck did you do it?"

"I don't remember a thing about it," Don said. "Must have been when I was trying to get into the pilothouse." Tubby came over and began to help him spread the ointment. Without looking at him, Don said: "I heard you saved the *Mallard*, Tub. Thanks a lot."

"That didn't amount to anything. I couldn't ever stand to see the old *Mallard* go up in smoke. She's still the best boat of her size on the coast, for my money."

"Shenrock's going to get her," Don said.

Tubby shook his head vigorously. "Like heck Shenrock is. Fishing's getting better every day and you've got a full month to go and then some."

"I made good last week," Don said. "But not good enough even if it stays that way clear to the end of the season."

"All we've got to do is take a little ice aboard and try it off Big Bank," Tubby said. "The cohoes are starting to show up there strong."

"You mean you'll come back with me?" Don asked him.

"Sure, why not?" He looked at Don's hands. "It'll be a few days before you do your stuff with those, anyway."

"You don't have to come just for that," Don said. "I'll make out."

"Don't be a sap. I've been hoping right along to get back to the *Mallard*. You can ask Happy."

Don held out one of his grease-smeared hands. "I'm sorry I acted so lousy, Tub."

"Heck," Tubby said. "I didn't have to get all hot and bothered about it the way I did."

Tubby brought his gear back aboard the *Mallard* that night, and early the next morning they pulled out for Big Bank tied alongside the *Falaise*. They had finished breakfast and the sun was up before they came to the Bank. Don went out on deck to steer from the trolling cockpit of the *Falaise*. In a little while Red came up and sat with him. It was a clear morning, without wind. Red pointed almost due south. "There's Canvasback Island," he said. Don followed the direction of his finger and saw a small, bare, rocky island that seemed to be six or eight miles away. "We go down that way once in a while," Red told him. "But not often. I figure the best part of the Bank for us is all pretty well north of the course we're on now."

"Between Canvasback Island and Snag Island a guy can get some kind of a fix," Don said.

"That's right, when you can see 'em; and there's the two mountains on Pendennis Island, they're usually the best bet, especially when you can see the mainland mountains as well. Seems kind of tough at first, but after a little while every little hump gets to mean something to you and you get so you can recognize the rips from the way they form up."

"You troll by the chart all the time, don't you?" Don asked.

"Pretty nearly. Sometimes, on a clear day, we get kind of lazy and don't pay much attention. But mostly we're on the compass and checking our times between markers. That way you know right where you are when you run into fish and you can count on hitting the same spot again, even in a fog."

"Sounds like we're starting it kind of late in the season," Don said.

"You'll be okay. Tubby's taken a bunch of courses off Tom's charts and soon as you've trolled those a few times you'll get the feel of it. We'll be in sight of you most of the time, but you want to hunt around a bit for yourselves, too."

"Because we're fishing shallow, you mean?"

"That's right. We've been getting our fish deep pretty near all season, but that don't mean we haven't been passing up something. Likely we have. There's some ten-fathom water over on the west side of the Bank, but mostly we've stayed away from that."

"Is that where Old Cowbells fishes?"

"Jake Heron?" Red laughed. "I doubt he knows where he is, most of the time. I'm pretty sure he hasn't got a good chart aboard. But he keeps his spoons working for him and he always gets some fish. I kind of admire the old guy."

"He's one boat that can't fish any deeper then we can," Don said. "So if he gets fish we ought to be able to."

"Sure you can. You'll outfish him a mile if you keep track of yourselves. Watch everything— tide and wind and time of day and, most of all, where you're at when you hit 'em."

Red looked down toward Canvasback Island again, then sighted back over his shoulder at Pendennis Island and the mainland mountains. "We'll be fishing in about ten minutes," he said. "Look, Don, in case I don't get another chance to tell you. I'm going to make a trip to town next week, to look at a new engine."

Don looked at him. "Right in the season? Won't it wait?"

"I'm going on the Union boat. Tom'll keep fishing the *Falaise*. I want him to have her alone for a while."

"How long will you be gone?"

"Inside of a week. Tom'll be fine. I'd just like to be sure you guys were around, though, so he'll have some company without having to go look for it."

"You mean you want us to stay close?"

Red shook his head. "Not so anybody could notice it. Just happen to be around. You will be anyway, so long as you're fishing Big Bank. Look, Don." Red's voice was almost pleading. "It's pretty important. Ever since that argument about the Japs Tom's been just like he always was. He was thinking and acting two jumps ahead of me right through that whole business yesterday. A week on his own right now, without me around, might be just all he needs to set him right for keeps."

"I get it," Don said. "You don't have to worry. We'll be there."

Red stood up. "I'll feel a lot better for that," he said. "I know Tom's going to be okay, but if anything did go haywire, I sure wouldn't want to have to live with myself."

Tom Moore and Tubby came out of the pilothouse. Tubby had a chart in his hand. "May as well cut loose and get fishing," Tom said. "Tubby knows more about the Bank than I do now.

Tubby grinned. "Enough to start looking for trouble, anyway," he said. "There's a few places out here where I figure I can hang us on bottom at ten fathom."

"Every time you find a new place to hang up it'll be worth a hundred bucks to you," Red told him. "That's the only way a troller ever learns his ground."

Five minutes later their lines were fishing. "Two sixty-six magnetic for forty minutes," Tubby said, "and we ought to bring South Hump on Mount

Queen. Then three zero four magnetic and hold it for around two and a half hours."

Don steadied the *Mallard* to the bearing. "Aye, aye, Cap'n Cook," he said. "She's right on the nose."

21

The first week of fishing Big Bank passed smoothly and quickly. Don and Tubby found themselves catching cohoes almost from the start, especially on the pig lines, and they ran in with a good load on Tuesday evening. Old Jake Heron sold his fish just ahead of them and they were able to see that they had more than double his catch.

They pulled out of Hardnose Cove long before daylight on Wednesday morning, fished through Wednesday, tied up with the *Falaise* over Wednesday night, fished Thursday, and ran in Thursday night with a still better catch. "We're on our way," Tubby had said. "That pickup comes from getting to know the grounds; there aren't any more fish around than there were earlier in the week." Their catch was down a little on Saturday night, but Tubby was still optimistic and confident. He made Don feel that there was once more plan and purpose in all they were doing.

Red had arranged himself a ride to town in a fishpacker that pulled out on Sunday. He told Don before he left: "I'll likely be back before the end of the week, but if everything's going okay, I might stretch it a bit. If Tom seems worried about anything, send me a wire. If I don't hear I'll know it's all smooth sailing and stay out of the way to give him a real run on his own.

The *Falaise* and the *Mallard* pulled away from the Cove together on Sunday evening, so as to be on the grounds and ready to fish first thing Monday morning. Don and Tubby and Tom had breakfast together before daylight on Monday. Tom seemed happy and eager to start fishing. Don asked him. "Where you going to work today, Tom?"

"Right in the old slave-run, cutting thirty fathoms along the slope close as I can," Tom said. "Course One out till I'm off North Hump, Course Two southward on the other side. That should bring me in sight of you by early afternoon. We can have mug-up then and one or other of us should know something good for the evening."

"We'll watch for you," Don said. "What if she comes up to blow?"

"She won't," Tom said, "not today. But if she does, you guys hit for the Hole. Don't take any chances. I'll ride out anything within reason, but if it looks anyways tough I'll be in there right behind you, quicker than I would if there were two of us aboard."

"Okay," Tubby said, "we'll do that. But don't you take chances either. It's getting on for fall now, and when she does come on to blow she'll likely mean business. This California spell can't last forever."

Tom smiled. "When did you ever see me taking chances?" he asked.

Fifteen or twenty minutes later the *Falaise* cut loose and Don and Tubby watched her on her way through the early dawn light. They saw Tom lower his poles and heard the diesel slow to trolling speed, then were busy about their own affairs.

During the previous week Tubby had hung them on bottom half a dozen times with only ten or twelve fathom of line out. Each time he had checked time and bearings closely against the chart and found no recorded sounding of less than twenty fathoms anywhere near where they had hit. By plotting these discoveries on his chart and tying them in with the few shallow soundings already there, he had at last established what seemed to be a wandering crest of shoal water toward the westerly side of the Bank. During Sunday afternoon he had worked busily to plot out a series of short courses that followed this wavering line as closely as possible. Now he brought the chart and showed it to Don.

"We'll likely hang up some more," he said. "But I've set the courses a fraction west of every place we've hit before. If they're right and we follow 'em close enough, our deep spoons should be right down there all the way."

They had their lines out, but there was still very little light and Don had to use a flashlight to see the chart clearly. He realized only slowly what a painstaking job Tubby had done. Tubby waited while he followed the thing out.

"Gee, Tubby," Don said at last. "You sure have been using your head. It looks to me like we ought to be able to show 'em all up when the run really comes in."

Tubby laughed. There had been a note of genuine admiration in Don's voice that he had seldom heard applied to himself. "It won't be that good," he said. "The boys'll be picking 'em up along Pendennis Island and out by Hideaway Rocks any time we're making a killing here. But we shouldn't have to take a back seat all the time."

That was the day the big run first hit the Bank. Don remembered it afterwards as a confused welter of gleaming fish—fish on every line, fish in the checkers, in the scuppers, in the holds, and on the hatch covers. One or two even slithered forward, through the pilothouse and into the engine room. By the time the sun was high and the take had slacked off they had fish enough to use all their ice and practically fill the second hold. Even at noon there were fish breaking around them and the lines were still catching a few.

The *Falaise* came back to them at about three o'clock in the afternoon, and by that time they had the boat tidy and the decks washed down. Tom Moore brought the *Falaise* alongside and they tied together. "Did you get 'em?" he asked.

"Boy," Don said, "did we ever!" He lifted the forward hatch. "There's the overflow. We've got our load in the other one. How did you make out?"

"Not that good," Tom said. "I stayed deep too long. But I thought you guys'd make a clean-up soon as I saw what was happening."

Don and Tubby climbed aboard the *Falaise*. They were both tired and more than ready to eat, but very happy.

"Did you see anyone else?" Tubby asked when they had the food on the table.

"Only old Jake in the *Blue Grass*," Tom said. "He followed me all morning, but I lost him on the way back. The old boy was fishing outside me, too; must have been over forty and fifty fathom water most of the time, and he didn't seem to be catching much."

"When did you first find the cohoes?" Don asked.

"I saw 'em jumping on the way up, but I didn't really catch on to it then. I was pulling spring salmon pretty good anyway, but I began to get cohoes after I turned on to Course Two."

"Tubby show you his chart?" Don asked.

"I saw him working on it yesterday. Why?"

"He'll have to show you," Don said. "I'll go fetch it."

He came back with the chart and passed it over to Tom. Tom studied it for a few moments, then whistled. "Looks like you've got something there, Tubby," he said. "Those the courses you fished today?"

"That's right," Tubby said. "We wandered some as we kept hitting fish, but by and large we stayed with it. You think there's a ten-fathom line all along there?"

Tom shook his head. "I know for a fact there isn't. We've trolled across it at twenty fathom and more too many times. Like here," he pointed to where two of Tubby's soundings were spaced well over a mile apart.

"We got our best fishing there," Don said. "Right off the northerly soundings."

"It's a pinnacle," Tom said. "We've laid thirty

fathom courses north and south of it. Same with the other one. I'm not too sure about the rest, though."

They ate in silence for a little while, then Tom said: "You better set yourselves up to fish right around those pinnacles instead of just along one side. It'll give you more good water."

"That adds up," Tubby said. "But if tonight's fishing's like it was this morning, we're going to have to run in with our catch ahead of time. Those fish in the forward hold won't keep without ice, and anyway, we'll have a load."

"No need of that," Tom said. "I can ice those and what you get tonight and we can both run in tomorrow night."

They did it that way, and Don was glad because it meant that Tom wouldn't be alone on Big Bank with the *Falaise*. When they got to the Cove and sold their fish, they found that the other boats had done almost as well along Pendennis Island. Over Wednesday and Thursday the fishing was just as good, and the *Falaise* ran in with them on Thursday night, again carrying part of their catch. Tom was at a considerable disadvantage in working the big boat alone, so he had ample room for his own two-day catch and the *Mallard*'s overflow.

On Friday Tubby said: "I don't think we ought to let him do it for us. You know, he could stay out four or five days straight if he wanted and put in a lot more fishing time."

"I know," Don agreed. "But Red did say to stay fairly close to the *Falaise* and Tom says he'll take packer's rates on the fish he carries for us."

"Still ain't right," Tubby said. "The guy's too good-natured."

"Well," Don said, "I'll ask him again."

But when they tied alongside the *Falaise* for a mug-up that afternoon, Tom just laughed at Don's suggestion. "Look," he said, "Red and I have made pretty good all season. Right now I'm catching 'way more fish than we'd figured I could while Red was away. Money isn't everything. When you've got enough to get by on, it isn't even very important."

"Sounds fine the way you say it," Tubby told him. "But I still don't feel right about it. It's catching us 'way more fish than we would be on our own and catching you 'way less. We get more fishing time than we should, you get less."

"So what?" Tom asked him. "We like each other's company, don't we? We get a chance to rest and relax and act like human beings, running into the Cove and back out again, don't we? We've got three people to cook and steer, instead of one, and three people's ideas to think about and talk about. That means more to me than a few dollars' worth of fish. So let's forget it. If I figured money was the main issue, I likely wouldn't be fishing anyway." Tubby started to say something, but Tom stopped him. "Have a heart, Tubby. When a man asks you to forget something, forget it. Talk about something else."

Tubby grinned. "Okay, Tom. Whatever you say."

"Tom," Don asked, "are you going to stick with fishing? Year in, year out, I mean? Like Red does?"

Tom thought for a moment. "Could be," he said. "I don't know why not. It's a good life, it pays pretty good money, and I like it. But more than likely I'll get ambitious again in a few years' time and go work twice as hard at something that pays a few cents more, or even a few cents less if it looks kind of promising."

"You're the kind that could do a managing job," Tubby said. "One of those where they make real dough."

Tom laughed. Don could see he was feeling very good, easy with himself, comfortable and interested. "No," he said. "I doubt if I'll want to go back working for anybody. Red and I have talked about spreading ourselves in the fishing business—building a good big packer, maybe, and trying to build up from there to a fleet. Or something like that. Look at what a fisherman's got. He's his own boss for one thing. He's free to move around all the water from Boundary Bay to Prince Rupert, through all the islands, up and down all the inlets, a couple of hundred miles out into the Pacific if he feels like it. He's always seeing new people and new places. Dozens of times Red and I have run into some harbor overnight and found a little logging outfit or an old trapper or a prospector or even some old retired guy who treated us as if we were royalty. There's really fine people all up this old BC coast once you get away from roads and cities."

He paused and Tubby said, "There's plenty in the fishing to keep a guy thinking, too."

"You're darn right there is," Tom agreed. "It gets hold of you, too. I don't think I'd be satisfied to stay just with the fishing end, nor Red either, but that's not because there isn't plenty to it. A man'd have to fish a lot of years to know the game as well as Happy does, for instance. But that's in a man's make-up. You've got boats in your make-up, Tubby, and maybe fishing too, so you'll stay with it. Don hasn't, not the same way. Don'll find something else before he settles down for life; something in the woods, maybe, or he might go back to school and learn a profession."

"You said that once before," Don said. "I've been thinking about it and I think I know more what you mean now. But why wouldn't I like all the things about fishing the same way you do?"

"You do like a lot of them," Tom said. "You like seeing new people and new places, you like being your own boss and being out of doors, you even like being on the water and around boats. But your mind doesn't take right hold on fishing the way it does on some things. I've heard you talk about trapping and hunting and it's different from when you talk about fishing."

"Seems a heck of a note," Don said, "for a guy to get himself a boat like the *Mallard* and then quit cold after one season."

"You don't have to do that," Tom told him. "You might fish two or three seasons with the *Mallard* before you make a change. You might suddenly get interested in fishing the way Tubby is and stay with it all your life. It's just I don't think you will. I think you'll move on to something else that's got a real pull for you."

"You could be right," Don said. "But I sure don't know what it would be."

Tom laughed again. "No reason you should. You've got a lot of good years ahead of you to figure that one out. There's lots of men don't come to what they're really meant to do until they're twenty-five or thirty and most of them are all the better for having shopped around a bit first." He looked at his watch. "We better get to fishing again if we want to go in with a full load tomorrow night."

22

Tom Moore had wired Red on Thursday about the big run of cohoes. The answer was waiting for him when they tied up on Saturday night and he showed it to Don and Tubby. "Go catch them yourself," it read. "I'm having me a time in the bright lights. See you around the end of next week. Be good and work hard. Red."

"What kind of a partner do you call that?" he asked. But Don could see that he wasn't worrying at all at the prospect of another week on his own. That first week had been an easy one, with nothing more than light westerly breezes in the afternoons.

The fishing had been steadily good all through, and there had been more boats than usual out at Big Bank; over Friday and Saturday at least half a dozen besides the *Falaise* and the *Mallard* and the *Blue Grass*. But through the whole of it Don had not been able to notice a sign of any doubt or worry in Tom's mind. Not only that; Tom had seemed fully as capable as Red himself in handling the *Falaise* and making decisions. He spoke of it to Tubby soon after they started fishing on Monday morning.

"You know, Red sure figured it out right when he decided to leave Tom on his own for a while. There's so much difference between the way he is now and the way he was when we first tied up with them at Starbuck River that it's like two different guys."

"He sure is different," Tubby agreed. "He even looks bigger and stronger."

"What gets me," Don said, "is the way he takes hold. We're supposed to be watching out for him, but it feels more like he's watching out for us most of the time. And that first week we were out here it seemed more like he was steering Red than the other way around."

"Sure," Tubby said, "but Red tries to make it that way. He always gives way to anything Tom says."

"When we first knew them Tom didn't use to say anything hardly. That night he tied into Jimmy

Hailon and Dave was the first time I've ever heard him talk out in a bunch of fellows, and he's been different ever since."

"Did you hear Jimmy'll be out of hospital this week?"

Don nodded. "And Dave's gone to town."

"Wonder if they'll team up again," Tubby said.

"I doubt it. Jimmy's not a bad little guy, but Dave's got nothing. The way he took care of himself and left Jimmy out there after the explosion was plain yellow."

"A guy can get confused in a setup like that," Tubby said thoughtfully. "It don't necessarily mean he's yellow."

For the next hour they were pulling fish steadily and there was little time for talk. When the take slacked off a little, Tubby said, "If she lasts out the week like this, we'll have old Shenrock beat."

Don shook his head. "It'll take more'n that. Pretty near another two weeks after this one."

"You could let me put my share in. Then this week'd do it."

"You mean it'd be like you taking a half share in the boat? Do you want that, Tub?"

"I sure do, if you'll let me buy in."

"You'd want it even if the fishing kept good for another month and I had plenty to take care of old Shenrock? You aren't putting up the idea just to help out?"

"Look," Tubby said, "I like this old *Mallard*. If the fishing stays good that long, I'll be offering to buy you right out."

Don laughed. "I'd tell you to go chase yourself. But, no kidding, I might take you up on that other, Tub. I don't see why it wouldn't be just as good if we had even shares in the boat."

"Think it over," Tubby said. "The offer's open any time."

The fishing held and the weather held until Thursday evening. The *Mallard* and the *Falaise* ran out to Big Bank together early Friday morning and separated before sunrise. Many other boats were out there, but most of them fished the easterly slope of the bank. No one else seemed to have found Tubby's ten-fathom pinnacles and ridges, though Jake Heron's *Blue Grass* sometimes fished near them and sometimes well beyond them to the west. Don and Tubby put out their lines and picked up their first markers as the dawn light showed behind the mainland mountains. The light grew and the water became silver gray, moving with a slight, smooth swell. Fish were taking and both Don and Tubby were busy, not talking except when they had to. Don watched the water. There was a tide rip a little ahead and he saw the swirls and slashes of feeding fish in it. A cohoe jumped against the silver water, twice, clear out and falling back on his tail, traveling south. Don found himself thinking of his trap line up Shifting Valley, and wondered why. Then he knew it was because there was something of fall in that morning's light and in the southward-traveling salmon jumping against the cold glint of the water. The thought was good, not bad. It would be good to see Joe Morgan's farm on the Starbuck again, good to kill a fall buck for the house, good to get his gear together and make the first trip up Shifting River in the canoe.

Don looked at the silver light on the salmon that were piling up in the checkers, the boxes built just forward of the cockpit where they left the fish until there was time to clean them and stow them. He liked the wet shine of the fish, clear and unbroken as though they were still alive. He liked the smell of them, a sharp smell but less sharp than that of fresh spring salmon. There would be salmon in the Starbuck now, on their way up to spawn already— sockeyes and humpbacks and springs, even a few cohoes, perhaps some of them fish that had passed within sight of the *Mallard*'s spoons. Just for a moment there flashed into Don's mind a realization of how completely dependent he was upon his country's yield of fish and fur and game. He recognized the parallel between taking the natural increase of his trap line and taking the natural increase of the salmon; it was a satisfying thought at first, then a worrying one. On his trap line Don was responsible for guarding the natural increase, for balancing his catch against it. Here on the fishing grounds he had no such direct responsibility, no way of checking anything or balancing anything.

His line of thought was broken quite suddenly as he looked again at the fish in the checkers. Their shine was no longer silver, but blood-red. Don looked to the east and saw a great red sun breaking clear of the mountains. Almost in the same moment he noticed an increase in the *Mallard*'s roll and the first cold edge of wind from the south. The water was red and gold from the rising sun, but its smoothness was gone, broken to little waves on the backs of the swells by that wind from the south. He heard Tubby say: "She's going to storm, Don, and quick. I say we better get out of here."

For the first time Don noticed a line of black clouds across the southern sky. Without hesitation he reached for the controls and speeded up the motor. "We'll take the lines in on the run," he said. "It'll take us two hours to make the Hole from here and we're going to need all the start we can get."

For the next little while they worked furiously. All the boats within sight had raised their poles and speeded up to run in. The sun disappeared behind clouds and the wind freshened in squally gusts. By the time they had the fish stowed and everything secured the storm was on them, driving rain and picking spray from the whitecaps. Standing in the pilothouse, Don said, "What about Tom?"

Tubby pointed northwestward. Don looked and saw the *Falaise* coming down toward them, almost abeam on the port side. He grinned. "Looks like he was worrying about us, too. Kind of nice at that."

As they watched, the *Falaise* swung round and began to run on a course parallel with their own, about two hundred yards away.

"I'm sure glad he's going in, too," Tubby said. "Coming up with the sun like that she's going to be a honey of a blow. Look at that *Falaise* ride them. You'd almost think she likes it."

"He's cut back to our speed," Don said. "That's one awful white guy, that same Tom Moore."

It was a short-breaking, hard-hitting, untidy sea, chopping against the flow of the tide, throwing and tossing the *Mallard* without any pattern or rhythm. Short waves slopped over the stern, hit the starboard side and even the bow. Don tried to ease the boat through them, but finally gave up and let Tubby take the wheel. "See if you can do better," he said. "You couldn't do worse. Nobody could."

"'Tisn't you, Don. It's the way they're breaking," Tubby said. But he took the wheel and the *Mallard* seemed easier for it. The wind grew loud in the rigging and there was an intermittent splatter of spray against the pilothouse door behind them.

"There's more corning," Tubby said. "But we'll be in before the worst of it."

Nearly two hours later they passed through the narrow entrance to the Hole and on into the quiet water beyond. The *Falaise* came through right behind them. "Like a good dog rounding up an old cow," Don said. "That Tom can sure handle his boat. You ain't so bad yourself, Tub."

"I've had all I want of that weather," Tubby said. "I'm good and glad to be in where it's quiet. The *Mallard's* okay, but there's too many things can happen to a little boat in that kind of sea."

A dozen or more boats were anchored in the Hole ahead of them. "Looks like everybody beat us in," Don said.

"We were fishing farthest out," Tubby said. "Unless... Say, Don, did you see Old Cowbells out there?"

Don shook his head. "Don't see him in here, either. He must have stayed in at the Cove."

"Could be. But it's not like him to stay in. I doubt if he could have figured the weather ahead. There was no gale warning before we pulled out."

They watched Tom Moore drop anchor, then Tubby ran the *Mallard* alongside the *Falaise*. Tom was out waiting for their lines. He asked at once, "See anything of Jake Heron?"

"No," Tubby said. "We figure he must have stayed home."

"We better find out if anyone else saw him," Tom said. "And quick" He was sliding the *Falaise*'s dinghy over the side. "I'm going round the other boats and ask."

Ten minutes later Tom was back. He climbed aboard without speaking. "Is he out?" Tubby asked.

"He started out," Tom said. "Several of them saw him. But they figure he turned back into the cove. Johnny Eliot says that some boats picked up a gale warning and turned back. He thinks maybe the *Blue Grass* did." Tom thought for a moment, then shook his head. "'Tain't good enough," he said, "no matter how you look at it. I've got to get back out there and look for him. The *Falaise* is the biggest boat in here."

"Okay," Don said. "When do we start?"

"You don't," Tom said. "It's my headache."

"Like heck it is," Tubby told him. "Ten chances to one you couldn't do anything alone if you did find him. With three of us and the *Falaise* we can handle anything, if he's still afloat."

"Something in that," Tom said. "Drop your hook and I'll get this one started. Haul the dinghy aboard, Don."

23

The *Falaise* came out of the entrance to the little harbor straight into three backbreaking swells, steep and high and short. The first tossed her bow to the sky, flipped under her stern and sent her sliding down into the narrow trough. She rose to the second; Tom swung her a little as she rode the crest, but the third one caught her, poured over the forward deck, and crashed in solid green against the pilothouse windows. Tom had throttled her back before the first one hit, but his face was set as they came out of the third and into the wind-flattened water beyond.

"That ain't the way it's meant to happen," he said. "The old *Falaise* hasn't taken one green since I've known her."

"Those were short, what I mean," Tubby said. He was braced hard against a corner of the pilothouse. "Seemed like there wasn't twenty feet between the crests and I'm darn sure it was twenty feet down into the troughs. We must have been right over the bar."

"We were," Tom said. "Six fathom at low water. She was breaking clear from the bottom. Look at the sand." He pointed to a little pile at the corner of one of the pilothouse windows.

Don looked ahead over the gray and white waves, into the rain and spindrift, and thought of old Jake Heron afloat out there alone in his square-built cracker box of a boat. He couldn't be afloat, Don thought. Just one swell like the three the *Falaise* had hit would be enough to founder the *Blue Grass*, even if it didn't tear the cabin and pilothouse clear away from her. It wasn't too hard to imagine old Jake drowned. The gray-faced, silent old man would look little different after the sea had washed him and bleached and silenced him forever. He would still be gray and strange and shut away from the life of ordinary men. Tom shouldn't be doing this, Don thought, taking a chance on himself and the *Falaise* for an old fellow who was probably either safe in Hardnose Cove or drowned two hours ago. It didn't make sense, yet it was something a man was bound to do and bound to want to do.

"How're we going to find him?" Don asked.

Tom shrugged his shoulders. "Keep looking till we do find him, I guess. I'm running on course now, from the entrance of the Hole over to the northerly end of Big Bank. It's only a guess, but I figure the old man likely got his engine doused right at the start, when he was taking in his lines and raising his poles. If that's right, he'll be low in the water and drifting slow. He won't be past the end of the Bank. If we turn south when we hit the Bank and keep somewhere along by Tubby's ten-fathom line, we'll stand a chance of running on to him."

"If it happened that way," Tubby asked, "do you think he'd be still afloat?"

"No," Tom said. "I don't. I don't think that crazy crate could live ten minutes in this stuff without her motor. But some queer things can happen and there's a man's life tied up in it."

"If he had his motor," Tubby said, "he'd been to the Hole by now, no matter how far out he was fishing. And this course'll hold us north of the course he'd have been on coming in. We could run on him any place from here out."

"That's right," Tom said. "We may as well start looking as though we meant it. You to starboard, Don. I'll take it straight ahead. Tubby to port."

For the next half hour all three of them searched out over the wind-torn water and they talked very little. Don tried to imagine Jake Heron and the *Blue Grass* fighting a storm of this kind, but he couldn't. Neither the man nor the boat seemed built for heroism. He pictured to himself how the *Falaise* would look now, remembering how they had seen her on the run in from Big Bank, rolling and riding and sliding her way over the swells, showing the red copper paint of her bottom below the white of her sides, folding the crests under her, breaking the power out of them with the wide flare of her high bows.

He glanced at Tom. "How much longer?"

"Twenty-five minutes and we'll come on to the other course," Tom said. "I may have underestimated this wind, but we won't be far out."

Tubby spoke from the other side of Tom. "She's still freshening."

Tom nodded. "I know. I figured on that, too. But she can't come up much worse than this. Look at that spray drive! Soon as a whitecap breaks it's gone like steam."

"They ride easier than they did coming in," Tubby said. "Longer and more even."

"They'll be dirty over the Bank," Tom said. "Short and coming from every which way. It'll take some boat-handling to get him when we find him."

"Have you figured how you'll go at it?" Don asked.

"Sure," Tom said. "I've figured a hundred ways, but none of them will be the one. There's two cotton lines coiled up forward though, one's half-inch, the other's inch. You may as well bring those up, Don. I'll watch your quarter."

Don came back with the lines and Tom said: "Lifejackets, too. There's three Mae Wests Red picked up, you'll find 'em under the starboard bunk. And bring one of the old cork jobs from under the other bunk."

Don laid the lifejackets out on the bunk in the pilothouse and Tom nodded approvingly. "Nobody goes out on deck without one of those and a line around him," he said. "If we have to do any jockeying around out there, it's going to be plenty rugged." He looked at his watch. "Two minutes," he said, "and we make the turn."

Tom made his turn, through eighty degrees of the compass, and they were running almost due southeast, magnetic, with the wind quartering on the starboard bow. Tubby gave a sigh of relief and admiration as the *Falaise* settled to the new course. "You didn't let her pound," he said. "And she didn't take it over even once, not to count."

"She's a dry boat," Tom said. "And a honey to handle. She's meant to be safe in weather like this." He checked his watch again and checked the compass reading. "If we're going to find him on this course, it'll be inside the next fifty minutes."

They found him in twenty minutes. Watching to starboard Don caught a movement of darker gray against gray through the scud. The *Falaise* climbed a swell and just for a moment he saw the gray hull below the tips of the trolling poles he had seen at first. He was sure of what he had seen, but it was hard to believe that the *Blue Grass* could be still afloat in such a sea and harder still to believe that they had found her so easily. He said quietly to Tom: "Bring her up to starboard as fast as you can. He's right abeam of us now, maybe a quarter of a mile over. You'll see him when the next swell lifts us."

Tom began to swing the *Falaise*, peering past Don. The swell lifted them, slid past, and let them down into the trough. "Still there?" Tom asked.

"Just the tips of his poles that time," Don said. "Keep watching. You'll pick him up in a minute."

The *Falaise* lifted again and all three of them saw the little gray hull, very flat and dead on the water. A wave broke clear over her as they watched, but she came through still afloat. "It's him, sure enough," Tom said. "Looks like he's pretty near swamped though."

Tom eased the *Falaise* round carefully in a wide smooth circle that brought her back down-wind toward the *Blue Grass*. When they were close, Tom slowed the *Falaise* until she barely had steerage way, but there was no sign of life from the

Blue Grass. He blew the *Falaise*'s air whistle and still there was no answer. The *Blue Grass* had a sea anchor of some kind out, holding her bow into the wind, but she was almost awash, moving sluggishly to the swells, taking wave after wave over deck and cabin and pilothouse. They saw Jake Heron at last, a stiff, unmoving figure in the pilothouse. He was staring straight ahead, his gray face set and strained, and he gave no sign of having seen them.

"I'll run past him close as I dare," Tom said, "then circle and come back into the wind. Open the door and stick your head out as we go by, Don. See if you can get the old man to see us."

The *Falaise* swept down toward the *Blue Grass*, swinging and twisting on the swells at slowest speed while Tom fought the wheel to keep her straight. They passed within ten or fifteen feet and Don saw Jake clearly. The old man was sitting at the wheel of his boat, rigidly upright, staring straight ahead into the storm. Don saw his hands on the wheel, but they did not move. He shouted into the storm three times, each time louder than the last, but the *Falaise* swept on past and still Jake had not moved.

Don turned back into the pilothouse and slid the door shut. "He must be dead," he told Tom. "He didn't make any sign of having seen us."

Tom shook his head grimly. "Not dead," he said. "Frozen. I'll bet he's been hanging on like that ever since she took the one that did the damage."

"That boat can't last long," Tubby said. "She's liable to founder any minute. I can't figure what's holding her up unless there's enough wood in the hull to float the motor and the rest of the junk he had aboard."

"That's it mostly," Tom said. "That and air pockets under the bow and under the hatch cover." He reached behind him for one of the lifejackets and began to put it on. "Grab one, Don," he said. "Take the wheel, Tubby, and bring her round so we can come to him upwind. Make your turn plenty wide and keep her dead slow."

Don was fastening his lifejacket. "What are we going to do?" he asked. "That old tub wouldn't tow a hundred feet before she went under for keeps."

"I'll tell you while we're coming back to him," Tom said. "And listen close, both of you. If anyone of us slips up in this, we're going to be in trouble." He was watching the *Falaise*'s swing as he talked. "The *Blue Grass* won't tow, that's certain. And old Jake's frozen there in his pilothouse. He won't make a move to help himself because he's quit; he's let himself die while he's still alive." The *Falaise* rolled heavily in her turn. Tom reached for a handhold, steadied himself, and went on. "The only thing left is to take a line aboard him. It's mostly up to Tubby. Tubby, you're going to handle this boat tighter than you've ever handled a boat before. You've got to run her in dead slow and a whole lot closer to the *Blue Grass* than you think is safe. Watch for me to go aboard with the line and soon as you see I'm there, swing away into the clear. After that, hold as close as you can without taking another chance of being thrown against her. Get it?"

Tubby nodded soberly. "My part's okay," he said. "I don't like yours. You going to try and jump aboard with that rope?"

"Let me take the rope aboard" Don said. "I'm a whole lot younger than you are."

"Skip it," Tom said. "These are orders I'm giving you and there isn't much time. Don, you'll go aft to the cockpit, tie yourself in there, and handle the ropes for me. I'll go aboard with the half-inch. Have the heavy line tied to the end of that." Tom waved a hand aft. "On your way, and tie yourself into that cockpit."

Don picked up the two coils of rope, opened the pilothouse door, and went out into the storm. He made it aft to the cockpit, fastened the stern line around his waist, and settled himself so that he had room and freedom to move. He glanced forward and saw the *Blue Grass* about a hundred feet ahead of them. Tom came out of the pilothouse with an extra lifejacket slung over one shoulder. Don handed him the free end of the half-inch line and watched him tie it around his waist. "Lots of slack when I need it," Tom said. "And pull like a horse when I say to." He laughed and ducked his head as a shatter of spray drove across the deck. Don watched him go forward slowly and carefully along the deck until he was almost at the bow. Tubby was lining the *Falaise* just a fraction away from the port side of the *Blue Grass*, bringing her slowly up from astern.

Watching from the cockpit, soaked with spray, battered by the wind, Don felt his heart pounding and knew he was scared. There was less than twenty feet between the boats now and they were both plunging like wild things as the quick, high swells bucked under them. Ten feet away and the *Falaise*'s bow seemed to throw twenty feet higher than the swamped afterdeck of the *Blue Grass*. Don saw Tom Moore climb over the *Falaise*'s gunwale, find footing on the four-inch guardrail below, and crouch there, ready to jump. The *Falaise*'s bow crept up past the stern of the *Blue Grass*, only three or four feet away from her. The two boats lifted together on a heavy swell. Tom jumped. Don saw him land on the deck, pitch forward to his hands and knees, roll over, and crash against the pilothouse. He got up, looked back towards the *Falaise*, and held his right hand up with two fingers spread in the V sign.

Tubby let the *Falaise* fall away ten or fifteen feet from the *Blue Grass*. A wave swept over the little boat and Tom crouched behind the pilothouse and hung on to the mast. As the wave passed he turned, wrenched open the door of the pilothouse, and went in. It was a tiny pilothouse and Don could see him in there shaking the old man and talking to him. The old man tightened his grip on the wheel and shook his head violently. Tom spoke to him again, pulled at his hands, and suddenly they were struggling. Tom hit once, hard, and the old man went limp. Another wave swept over the *Blue Grass*, but Don could see that Tom was fitting the lifejacket over old Jake's shoulders and working on the fastenings. Then another wave came, the stern of the *Blue Grass* disappeared under it, her bow lifted, and Don found himself pulling half-inch line with the dead weight of two men at the end of it.

The line came in easily for a few feet, then the weight was dead astern and he could not gain an inch. He heard Tubby cut the motor right back and felt the *Falaise* lose way. "Gee, Tub," he thought. "Watch it. Don't let her swing broadside." But the rope came in fast and almost easily, and he could see Tom in the bright lifejacket, gripping the other jacket that supported old Jake. Then the pull was heavy again and Don hung on until the sweat started all over him. Tubby's hands were on the rope beside his, helping to take the strain, before he noticed the *Falaise* was going ahead again.

"I've kicked her ahead slow," Tubby was saying. "Had to to hold her into them at all."

They pulled together and Tom was suddenly very close, dangerously close under the heaving stern. He tried to shout something. Don told Tubby: "Make the slack fast, any place. Then hang on to my legs."

A moment later Don was face down over the stern, the inch line in one hand. Water poured over him, filled his nose and eyes, tore at his shoulders. He felt his fingers on Jake's lifejacket, gripped hard, and went under again. Somehow he got the rope around Jake's body, slung two half hitches on it, and pulled tight under his armpits. He yelled to Tubby as another one hit, and felt himself dragged back inboard. After that it was almost easy. They hauled Jake in first and let the old man lie, gray and unmoving, on the floor of the narrow cockpit. Then it was Tom's turn. He grabbed the gunwale as he came within reach of it and almost pulled himself aboard. For a moment he stood in the cockpit, gripping the edge and coughing salt water out of his lungs, then he turned to Tubby. "Pick her up to half speed," he said. "And hold her while Don and I get the old man forward. The quicker we get out of here, the better."

24

Don remembered the trip back to the Hole from the rescue on Big Bank as a mixture of dreariness and elation. After they had turned to run from it the storm was still drearily the same, tiresomely insistent and dangerous and uncomfortable, driving after the *Falaise*, rolling her, threatening to climb aboard her. He was soaking wet, and cold, standing beside an almost equally wet Tubby in the pilothouse. Tom Moore was down below, putting splints on old Jake's right arm, which seemed to be broken. The old man had come to himself and they could hear him groaning with pain even from the pilothouse.

After a little while Tom came up, wearing dry clothes. "I put more dry stuff on the bunk," he said. "Go wring yourselves out. I'd make coffee, but we couldn't keep a pot on the stove long enough to boil."

Below, old Jake lay on the bunk with his eyes closed, groaning a little whenever the boat lurched enough to move his arm. Don asked if he wanted anything and he opened his eyes and looked at them both. "Thanks, boys," he said. "Thanks." Then he turned away and closed his eyes again.

Tubby nodded toward the pilothouse. "That," he said, "is a man, and a real man, what I mean. A person sure can get a guy all wrong the first time he meets him."

Don didn't answer for a moment. He was thinking it hadn't even seemed very difficult with Tom there on top all the time. Yet it was so nearly impossible all along the line that most men wouldn't even have tried it. "Did you notice how it felt to be working for him?" he asked Tubby. "As though there couldn't be any other way of doing it and it couldn't go wrong?"

"You're darn right, I did," Tubby said. "Do you think I could have laid this old boat within a couple of feet of the *Blue Grass* if it hadn't been for the way he put it up to me and the way he took it for certain I would? If Tom said to flap my arms and fly home to Bluff Harbor, I believe I could do it right now."

From then on they could feel the strength of what they had done. It became a shared thing between the three of them, a bond of experience far stronger than the simple realities of driving wind and drenching spray, of straining arms and plunging boats and shattering waves and the nearness of death. As they dropped anchor in the quiet of the Hole, Tom said: "Let's keep it simple when the boys come aboard. Just that we got a rope to him in time and it wasn't so bad out there after all—you know." Both Don and Tubby did know. The truth of what had happened was simple and easy because it had worked out. You couldn't tell, except perhaps to Red Holiday, why it had been possible at all, much less why it had been simple and easy.

The storm lasted into the night but died away in the hours before dawn. Old Jake had been comfortable during the night. Johnny Eliot, who had an industrial first aid certificate, had checked Tom's splinting of the arm and changed it a little, but the fact that the boat was lying in sheltered anchorage was what really made the difference. At breakfast the old man was almost cheerful. He remembered little of what had happened except that a big wave had washed over the stern of the *Blue Grass* and swamped her engine, and he had managed to throw out a sea anchor, then shut himself into the pilothouse. He asked Tom what had happened to the *Blue Grass.*

"I'm afraid she's gone," Tom told him. "You had insurance on her, didn't you?"

The old man nodded. "Sure had," he said. "Spent a mint of money on it too, but I reckon it was worth every penny."

"How about cash?" Don asked. "Didn't you have any aboard?" All the trollers knew that Jake insisted on cash payment for his fish and hadn't much faith in banks.

The old man chuckled and patted his belly. "Right around here," he said. "Eleven hundred and ninety-two dollars and sixty-five cents. Any time St. Peter sends for Jake Heron in a hurry he won't come empty-handed."

After that he said little until Tom started the *Falaise*'s engine to run him up to the hospital at Whale River. Then, as Don and Tubby were climbing back aboard the *Mallard*, he said: "Jake Heron ain't no lawyer when it comes to talkin', boys. But don't think he don't know what you done. I don't reckon I'll be fishin' no more this season, but any time you're down around the Fraser Valley, me and the missus'll make you mighty welcome."

"We'll be there one day," Don told him. "And we'll be seeing you next summer, in the new boat."

They watched the *Falaise* until she passed

out of sight through the entrance to the harbor. Then Tubby said, "What now?"

"More fish," Don said. "There's gas enough to fish at Big Bank till dark and run back to the Cove tonight. Then we'll pull out with Tom again tomorrow morning."

Red Holiday came back from town three days after the storm, and the *Mallard* and the *Falaise* fished together steadily on Big Bank until the cohoe run began to fade nearly four weeks later. The run had held up strongly in day after day of good fishing until a mild southerly blow brought several days of heavy rain. After that, the fish disappeared and for three or four days they caught little. Then Red said one evening: "Looks like we've had it. What do you say, Don?"

"I've been thinking we could do this well down in the Gulf," Don said. "The *Mallard*'s paid off and Tubby's got his stake. Why don't we all go down and tie up in the River for a fall deer hunt? I know Uncle Joe and Aunt Maud'll be glad to see us."

"Sounds good to me," Red said. "What do you say, Tom?"

"Couldn't be better," Tom said. "I'm just as ready as Don is to get my feet on dry land again. And I could stand to eat a meal that wasn't cooked on the top of a galley stove."

So they started south the next day, traveling lazily on the fair tides, tying up overnight wherever seemed easiest. Don began to feel the excitement of homecoming soon after they turned from Johnstone Strait into Discovery Passage, and he settled himself in the cockpit to pick out familiar landmarks and get the feel of fall from the near-by land. It was a warm afternoon, sunny and mild, but he could see the smoke of fall slash burning beyond the Narrows, and there was gold of maple and scarlet of dogwood all through the dark green of fir and hemlock up the hillsides. Red came back and sat with him.

"Well," he said, "how was the north? Good as you expected?"

"Okay," Don said, "I guess. I learned something anyway, even if I didn't make a killing."

"You saved your boat in a bad season," Red told him. "And you had a hand in saving two lives. What more do you want?"

"Nothing," Don said. "It was okay." He watched the hills in silence for a minute or more, then he asked: "Say, Red, do you think I should quit and not fish another season? Do you think I haven't got what it takes?"

"What do you think?" Red asked him.

"Me? I don't want to quit. Maybe I will sometime, but I'd as soon fish another season or two anyway. I guess I'll never be a fisherman alongside you and Tom and Tubby, but I know I can make out alongside most of the guys up there."

"That's all the answer you need," Red told him. "Sure you'll stay with it. You and Tubby make a good team. Next year you'll have steel lines and gurdey spools on the *Mallard* and you'll know the score. If there's fish around at all, you'll get your share."

"You don't think Tubby'd be better off without me?"

"No, I don't. Tubby's a good fisherman and he's real good with a boat. But there's plenty of things you've got that he hasn't. Tubby needs you a whole lot more than Tom Moore's ever going to need me again, but you don't see us planning to split up, do you?"

"You think Tom's okay now, for good?"

"I'm sure of it as I am of anything. Tom looks and acts and talks just the way he did when I first knew him, has done ever since that evening he said his say about the Japs. I got to see the doctor in Shaughnessy Hospital while I was in town and he said to forget from now on that Tom ever had any trouble. That's why I stayed away so long."

Don nodded slowly. "A person can feel the difference in him. There's something strong comes out of him and he doesn't even have to talk to make you feel it. That's how it was the whole time we were out after Jake Heron. That's what I tried to tell you about. Tubby could feel it, too."

Red smiled. "Leadership," he said. "That's what they used to call it in the army. Only half the time you couldn't tell which guys had it till the heat was on."

Tubby came back from the pilothouse and sat down on the after hatch. Tom Moore followed him a moment or two later.

"We'll catch the top of the flood in the Narrows," he said. "Should make your river around six o'clock, Don."

"Just right for supper at home," Don said.

"We'll eat aboard the boat and go up after," Tom told him. "Nobody wants the whole four of us for a meal without warning."

"You don't know Aunt Maud," Don said. "She can put a meal for a young army on the table in the time it takes to wash up ready for it. She'd be madder'n heck if we stopped to eat first."

Tubby was listening with his arms clasped around his knees. "That's right," he said. "Mrs. Morgan can whip up a meal quicker'n anyone I ever saw."

"We've got those steaks aboard," Tom said, "the ones we bought last night. We could take those up."

"I don't think I'll make home till tomorrow," Tubby said. "Gee, my old man's going to be sore when he finds I've earned more this summer than all his pay checks from the mill."

"Why's that?" Red asked.

Don laughed. "'Going yachting,'" he said. "That's what Tubby's old man calls fishing. 'Go ahead and take your summer cruise' was what he told Tubby when we were starting out. 'You'll come to working for a living yet.'"

"He's never really sore," Tubby said. "Just puts on a big act. But I like to hear him start on something like this."

"You won't have a chance to," Don said. "Yachtsmen are capitalists. They have to re-invest darn near all their earnings."

Tubby looked startled. "How's that?" he asked. "What do you mean? Income tax or something?" He saw that the others were laughing. "I get it," he told Don. "You've thought it over and you'll sell the *Mallard*."

Don shook his head. "No, not sell her. I'll let you come in on a half share is all. That right, Red?"

Red nodded. "That's right," he said. "And next May the whole four of us will be heading out together again. We'll make the *Mallard* and the *Falaise* high boats right through the season."